SQUEEGEE KID

ALSO BY S.E. TOMAS

Crackilton

Squeegee Kid

a novel by

S.E. Tomas

A CREATESPACE BOOK

1

It was October '96. The carnival season was over and I was stranded in Mobile, Alabama, where I'd been working for Conklin Shows.

I looked at the tire tracks in the gravel, where the show had been set up and started to panic. Shit, I thought. What the hell am I going to do?

All I had were the clothes on my back and a few bucks on me. The rest of my money was under my mattress, in the bunkhouse I'd been staying in all season.

Seeing as how I was totally screwed, the first thing I did was walk to the nearest payphone and call my mom in Edmonton, Alberta.

I hadn't talked to my mom in over four years. I figured that since I was in a jam, though, she'd be willing to wire me some money so that I could get to Florida and get my stuff out of my bunk.

There were payphones near the entrance to the fairgrounds. I went over there, picked up the phone and called my mom collect.

Luckily, my mom still had the same phone number. She agreed to accept the charges, which I took to be a good sign.

I knew that there was no sense in dancing around the issue, so I just straight-up asked my mom if she could send me some money.

"Oh, you need *money*," my mom said. "I should have known that's why you were calling, Jim."

"Mom, I'm sorry," I said, "but I'm stranded in Alabama. I didn't know who else to call. I've got no money on me. I'm here at the lot, in Mobile, and the show's gone. They left early today for some reason. I just need some money so that I can get to Miami, where they took the bunkhouses. I promise I'll pay you back."

Some of the bunkhouses actually weren't going to Miami; they were going to Dothan, Alabama. That spot, which ran through Halloween, was technically the show's last spot of the season. My boss, though, Greg Melnik, never played Dothan. It was a smaller lot than the one in Mobile, so the entire show couldn't play it. After Mobile, Greg always hauled all of his shit down to Conklin's winter quarters in Miami, so that's where my bunk was going.

All I was asking was for my mom to send me enough money so that I could buy a bus ticket. My mom wouldn't do it, though. "No way," she said. "I'm not sending you money. You can't just call me up out of the blue like this, just because you're stuck somewhere, and think I'm going to jump in my car and drive to Western Union. Anyway, why did you leave the lot? Why weren't you there when the show was leaving this morning?"

"Because I went to a hotel last night," I said. "We'd just torn down and the show had turned off the power and the water. I wanted to take a shower."

"Hmpf."

"So, you're not going to help me, then? You want me to hitchhike, I guess."

"I don't care what you do."

The next thing I knew, I was hearing dial tone. My mom had hung up.

"Bitch," I muttered.

I hung up the phone, and then immediately picked it up again and dialed a cab company—the same one that had just let me off. There was no point in sticking around the fairgrounds. There wasn't much around there. It was a rural area.

In a few minutes, the cab showed up.

I got into the backseat. "Take me downtown," I said.

In about twenty minutes, we were downtown.

"Where do you want me to let you off?" the cabbie said.

We were driving down what looked like the main drag.

"I don't know," I said. "Here's good."

The cabbie pulled over. I paid the fare, got out, and then started to walk down the street.

I had no idea where the hell I was going. I didn't even know where I was, other than that I was in downtown Mobile. I didn't know Mobile at all. I'd always come in and out of that town with the show. The night before, when I'd gone to the hotel, I'd told the cab driver, "Take me to the nearest hotel." I had no idea where the hotel was relative to the fairgrounds. It was dark. Everything we drove past in the car looked the same.

As I walked down the street, I told myself that I was going to have to look for a homeless shelter or a hostel. I was going to need a place to sleep for the night, and I sure as fuck wasn't going to be staying in a hotel.

As I walked, I heard someone calling my name all of a sudden. I turned and looked over my shoulder. "Oh, hey, Leon," I said.

Leon was a guy who worked on the show. Like me, he worked in one of Greg Melnik's games. I honestly didn't like the guy. He was a fighter-type; a bully. Of all the people on the show that I could have run into, Leon was probably the last person that I wanted to see.

"Hey," Leon said. "What are you doing downtown?"

"I'm looking for a shelter," I said.

"Huh?"

"The show took off, bud. We're stuck here."

Leon looked like he didn't believe me. He looked at his watch. "But it's not even eleven o'clock," he said.

"I know," I said. "Trust me, though. I was just at the lot. Everyone from the show was gone."

Leon sighed, and then looked at the ground. "I thought we'd leave at noon, like usual," he said. "I never heard Greg say that we were leaving early today."

"Neither did I," I said. "And he left really early, too. I got to the lot at ten. He'd already taken off."

In the harsh morning sun, Leon looked rough. He looked like he'd stayed up all night on a crack binge. In Mobile, crack wasn't hard to find. The dealers literally hung out right outside the fairgrounds. If you had any money on you, they'd force you to buy it. They'd rush at you, all at once, saying, "How much do you want?"

"So, what happened to *you* last night?" I said to Leon.

"I fell in," Leon said. "I went to leave the lot and those niggers rushed me at the gate. Shit, I wish I hadn't spent all my money. Do you got any money on you, Jim?"

"A few bucks. It's like I said, I'm looking for a shelter."

"I guess we better do that, eh?"

"Yeah. We'll need a place to stay until we can figure out how we're going to get the fuck out of here."

Leon and I started to walk down the street. The street had those trees that you saw in Mobile with the creepy-looking branches that seemed to grow sideways, rather than upwards, over the streets.

As we walked, we asked random people we passed in the street if they knew where we could find a shelter. We had no luck at first, but we eventually ran into someone who could help us—this old black broad.

This broad was a total Jesus freak, which, in the South, wasn't too hard to come by. She had this huge cross around her neck. Clutched to her chest was a bible.

The broad told us where the shelter was, and then gave us directions on how to get there. "My husband volunteers there once a week," she told us. "I bring his old clothes over there sometimes."

Yeah, I bet, I thought.

"All right," Leon said.

"Yeah, thanks," I said.

"Take care," the broad said. "And God bless."

Leon and I found the shelter. It was a brown brick building that looked almost like a community centre. It was located in sort of a remote area. It felt like we were on the outskirts of the downtown.

In front of the shelter, a bunch of old bums were sitting around, hanging out. Leon and I found out from the bums that we couldn't go into the shelter until later in the day.

Rather than hang around with these bums all day, or with Leon, I told Leon that I'd see him later, and then I just walked around downtown all day by myself.

In the early evening I went back to the shelter. The bums were all lining up to get in. I ran into Leon and joined him in the line.

As we were standing in line, I suddenly got an idea. I turned to Leon. "Hey," I said. "I just thought of something, man. We're Canadian citizens and we're stranded in a foreign country."

"Yeah," Leon said.

"Well, we should call the Canadian embassy."

I figured the Canadian embassy would have to get us back to Canadian soil. I had no problem calling them. I was in the United States legally. I had a work visa. Leon didn't need one because he was Native.

At first, Leon didn't want to call the embassy.

"Why not?" I said.

"I think we should just wait until Greg's in Miami, and then try to call him."

"Do you know his number there?"

"No, but we can look it up."

"OK. Assuming we get his number, do you really think he's going to help us? He didn't seem to care too much when he took off on us today. I'd rather call the embassy right now and just get the ball rolling."

Leon still didn't want to call.

"Well, I'm going to call," I said. "I'll just call on my own behalf, then."

Leon and I were now at the front of the line. We went into the shelter. I looked around. Everyone in the entire place was black. I was the only white guy there. Even the staff there were black.

The shelter had a phone that I could use. I picked up the phone, and then dialed the operator. "I want to talk to the Canadian embassy," I said.

"One moment, please," the operator said. Then she transferred the line.

Once I got through to the embassy, I was transferred a bunch of times. I finally got through to someone who could help me.

At first, the person wanted to know if I had any friends or relatives who could wire me money, so that I could get home on my own.

I almost laughed at the question. "No," I said. "I wouldn't be calling you guys if that was the case."

"Are you able to get any work in Mobile?"

"No. My work visa expired. I can't work. I've got no money. My employer took off on me and left me stranded here with only the clothes on my back. I'm in a homeless shelter right now. That's where I'm calling you from, by the way."

"OK. Well, have you tried contacting your employer?"

"No, he's on the road. There's no way I can get a hold of him right now."

"What's the name of your employer?"

"I'd rather not say."

Even though I was pissed off at Greg, I wasn't going to rat the guy out. That's all I needed—to get blacklisted on the carnival. I'd never work on a fucking show again.

I heard some typing.

"Please hold the line, sir," the broad said.

"Yeah, OK," I said.

After holding for about fifteen minutes, the broad came back on the line. She had me confirm my name, date of birth, and social insurance number.

"OK, so what happens now?" I said.

"We're going to process your case," the broad said. "You'll need to call us back in three days."

Great, I thought, as I hung up the phone. What the fuck am I going to do here for the next three days?

I was already so sick of Mobile. The only reason I'd even played the spot was so that I could get a ride with the show afterwards to Florida. I was planning on going to Santa's Enchanted Forest, which was a seventy-two day spot in Miami that started in October and closed right after New Year's. There had been no other reason for me to play Mobile. The spot had always been a blank. I'd never made any money there. Mobile wasn't that big of a town. And the people who came to the fairgrounds, the majority of whom were black, didn't spend much on the games. It was an extremely poor town.

Leon came over to me, as I was hanging up the phone. "What happened with the embassy?" he said.

"They're going to process my case," I said. "I've got to call them back in three days."

"All right. I think I'll call."

Leon called the embassy. The person he spoke to told him to call back in three days, too, apparently.

Shortly after we made our phone calls, the shelter served everyone some free food. I was starving. I hadn't eaten anything all day.

Leon and I got in the food line with all the other bums. We each took a tray and when it was our turn, we got served by the person behind the counter. The set-up was like in a high school cafeteria—there was somebody behind the counter serving the food and they just put whatever you wanted onto your tray.

That night I slept on a thin plastic mattress on a very hard floor.

As I stared up at the ceiling of the crowded, smelly room, I thought to myself, "Greg, you motherfucker."

2

The three days went by extremely slowly. When it was finally time to call the embassy back, I used the phone at the shelter again.

"We've processed your case," I was told by the person I spoke to at the embassy. "There's a bus ticket waiting for you at the Greyhound station in Mobile. You'll be leaving in two days for Toronto, Ontario."

I wasn't too happy to hear that I'd be going to Toronto. Even though I'd been there before with the carnival, I didn't know a damn person in that city who could help me out once I got off the bus. I had some phone numbers in my wallet, but these were just work acquaintances. I couldn't call any of these people up and just ask to stay at their place. And anyway, a lot of these guys were going to be hard up themselves. If they weren't collecting employment insurance, now that the season was over, they'd be living off savings or welfare.

I tried to explain this to the guy at the embassy. "I'm from Edmonton," I said. "Isn't there any way that you could get me back there, or at least to Calgary or something? There's no one who can help me in Toronto, once I get there. All my relatives are out west."

"I'm sorry," the guy said. "But we can only bus you as far as the nearest major Canadian city, which in your case is Toronto. If you want to get to Edmonton, or to any other Canadian city, you'll have to arrange that on your own."

I was obviously asking too much from the Canadian government. When I got off the bus in Toronto, I was just going to have to figure it out.

"OK, that's fine," I said.

The guy gave me the address for the bus station in Mobile. Then he told me the exact time of day that the bus would be departing.

I scribbled the information down on a piece of paper that the shelter staff had given me.

"Before I let you go, I just need to confirm your mailing address," the guy said. "Then I need to arrange a skill-testing question with you."

The mailing address, I knew, was so that the government could send me the bill for the bus ticket. I had no intention of paying back the government, but I obviously wasn't going to say that to this guy. I didn't have a mailing address, so I gave him my mom's address in Edmonton.

"What's the skill-testing question for?" I said.

"It's so you can claim your bus ticket," the guy said. "When you go to the Greyhound station, you'll need to go to Guest Services. You'll be asked to show some ID, and then you'll be asked to answer a pre-arranged question in order to get your ticket. In addition to the ticket, you'll also be given a food allowance for your trip."

We arranged the skill-testing question over the phone.

I was done talking with the embassy at this point, so I just passed the phone to Leon, who was standing next to me.

A few minutes later, Leon got off the phone. "We're going to be on the same bus," he told me.

Since Leon and I had no money, the staff at the shelter had to arrange transit for us to get to the bus station. When it was time to go there, the staff gave us a taxi voucher, and then called us a cab.

It was a really small bus station on the side of a road. When the cab pulled up to it, it almost looked like a little store or something.

Leon and I went inside the bus station and went straight to Guest Services. I was expecting a hassle, but as it turned out, the clerk wasn't too thorough. She didn't even ask to see our IDs. All she did was ask us for our first and last names, and then she went straight to the skill-testing questions.

"Mother's maiden name?" the clerk asked me.

"Hayes," I said.

"Spell that."

"H-A-Y-E-S."

The clerk handed me a piece of paper. "Please read and sign this form," she said.

I quickly skimmed the form. It just said that by signing my name, I was agreeing to reimburse the Canadian government for the bus ticket and for the food allowance that they were giving me for the trip.

Yeah, whatever, I thought, as I signed my name.

The clerk gave me my ticket and an envelope, containing the money. Leon then went through the same process. When he was done, we left Guest Services and went to go find our bus.

It was such a small bus station that there was only one bus outside. People were already lining up to board it. I looked at the front of the bus and saw that it was headed to Toronto. Leon and I got in the line.

We didn't have to wait too long to board the bus. Since we didn't have any luggage, we just showed the driver our tickets and hopped on.

I grabbed a seat at the front of the bus, as far away from the toilet as possible. Leon sat further back. Within a few minutes, the bus took off and got on some U.S. interstate.

There were a lot of layovers and transfers to other buses as we drove through the United States. It was a good thing the embassy had given me a decent-sized food allowance because almost everywhere we stopped, the only place to eat was the bus station, where the food was really expensive. I'd found this to always be the case, though, whenever I'd travelled by Greyhound. You could burn through a lot of money, eating at the bus station, if you wanted to eat well.

It was a really long and boring trip. We drove through some pretty dull-looking states. After a day on the bus, I just wanted to be in Toronto already. I was tired of sitting, and of sleeping in a seated position. I felt dirty. I'd showered at the shelter in Alabama, but I'd been in the same clothes for days.

The last U.S. city that we stopped in was Buffalo, New York. Then we were in Ontario. The whole trip took a couple of days. It was about a forty-hour bus ride.

We arrived in downtown Toronto, at Bay and Dundas, in the early afternoon. Leon and I got off the bus and immediately went our separate ways. I honestly didn't care what happened to the guy. I hadn't even sat with him on the bus at any point during our trip.

I left the bus station and started to walk down Dundas Street, towards Yonge Street. I knew exactly where I was going because I'd travelled to Toronto before by bus and was familiar with the area around the Toronto Coach Terminal.

At Yonge Street, which was a block away from the bus station, was the Dundas Street entrance to the Eaton Centre—a big shopping mall in the downtown core. I went into the mall and immediately started looking for a job. I knew that as soon as I got a job and started working, I'd be fine. I'd have money coming in. I just needed to find something quick.

In about fifteen minutes, I found a clothing store that was hiring. "Salesclerk wanted," the sign in the window said. "Apply within."

I'd never sold clothing before, but my line of thinking was that if I could sell teddy bears to grown adults on the carnival, I could sell clothes.

I went into the store and talked to the manager.

As we talked, the manager noticed the logo on my jacket. "Conklin Shows," he said. "You worked there?"

"Yeah," I said.

"What did you do there?"

"I worked in the games department."

"Oh, so you're a salesman?"

"Yeah, and a damn good one."

I'd only worked in a game for four and a half seasons, but I was pretty good at it already. My grosses were always high because I never shut up. I was always calling people into my game.

"Have you ever worked in retail?" the manager said.

I had to lie, here. "Oh, sure," I said. "Before I started working on the carnival, I worked in retail, back in Edmonton. That's where I'm from originally. I sold clothes, watches—all kinds of things."

"So, now you're in Toronto."

"Yeah, I actually just got off a Greyhound half an hour ago. I was down in the United States with the carnival and I got stranded in Alabama. I just need to get a job and get back on my feet right now."

The manager was impressed with my confidence and with my eagerness to find work. I didn't even have a resume on me, just the clothes on my back, and he hired me right there, on the spot.

"Great," I said. "When do I start?"

"Tomorrow," the manager said. "The job I'm hiring you for isn't at this store, though, it's actually at a store downstairs called Garage USA. The guy who owns that store also owns this store and three other stores in the mall. I'm the general manager. I do all the hiring and oversee all the stores."

The manager started to tell me about the position he'd just hired me for. "Just so you know, this job is full-time," he said.

"Good," I said. "I need something full-time. We should talk salary, though. What does this job pay?"

"Six eighty-five an hour, but you'll have the opportunity to earn a commission. Certain merchandise in the store are what we call 'big ticket' items. If you sell a big ticket item, you don't make the hourly wage for that hour, you collect the commission, which is fifteen percent of the sale price."

It sounded like a pretty good deal to me. On the show, I worked strictly on a commission basis, which meant that if I didn't gross anything in the game that I was working in, I didn't get minimum wage, I got jack shit. I was just happy to hear that I had a chance to earn a commission.

I might actually make some money here, at this crappy job, I thought.

We shook on the deal, and then the manager told me where Garage USA was in the mall. "It's closest to the Queen Street entrance," he told me. "If you go in through that entrance, and you go down the escalator to where the food court is, it's right there, in front of the escalator."

"Thanks," I said. "I'll find it."

I left the mall and walked out onto Yonge Street. I felt relieved. I'd been in Toronto for less than half an hour and I already had a full-time job.

My next mission was to find a place to stay for the night. It was still early, so I hung around the Eaton Centre for a while. In the late afternoon, I started to look for a homeless shelter.

It took me a while, but I finally ran into someone who knew the shelter system in Toronto. This guy had obviously stayed in the shelters himself because he knew which ones were the best ones to go to.

"You're too old for Covenant House," the guy told me. "Go to Turning Point."

"Where's that?" I said.

"It's on Wellesley, near Jarvis. Of all the shelters in the downtown core, it's probably the cleanest one."

The guy had to give me directions on how to get to Jarvis and Wellesley because I didn't know Toronto that well. I really only knew the area around the bus station and where some of the spots were that I'd played with the show.

"It's an old house that was converted into a shelter," the guy told me. "You can't miss it. It's really big. Just so you know, that double wooden door at the front of the building—that's not for Turning Point. That's for another institute or something. The door for Turning Point is on the side, along the fence."

"OK, thanks," I said.

"No problem."

It took me about twenty minutes to walk to the shelter from the Eaton Centre. I walked up Yonge Street to Wellesley Street, and then walked along Wellesley to the shelter. By the time I got there, it was dark outside. It was after six o'clock.

I spotted the fence the guy had told me about. I walked down the side of the building, by the fence, and found the door. "Turning Point for Youth," the sign said.

Outside the door was a buzzer and an intercom. I pressed the buzzer, and then looked up at the surveillance camera above the door. "Hello?" I said.

A guy spoke to me over the intercom. "Yes?" he said. "Can I help you?"

"Yeah, I'm wondering if I could stay here," I said. "I've got nowhere else to go."

There was a pause. I heard the sound of the door unlocking.

"OK," the guy said. "Come in."

I opened the door and went inside the shelter. Right where you came in was a big, square room enclosed in glass. It was an office area. It was obviously where the staff sat in the place. There was a window where you could go up and talk to the staff.

The guy who'd let me into the shelter had been sitting in the office area. He came to greet me at the door.

"I'm Andrew," the guy said. "I'm one of the staff here, at Turning Point."

"I'm Jim," I said.

"Nice to meet you, Jim."

Andrew had me come into the office to do an intake interview. The interview was really formal. I was asked a lot of questions. I was even asked to produce ID. Luckily, when I'd gotten stranded, I'd had my wallet on me, with all of my identification in it.

I wanted Andrew to know up front that I wasn't just some bum, looking for a free place to stay. During the interview, I told him about how I'd gotten stranded by the carnival in Alabama, and how I'd already found a job. My goal, I told him, was to get back on my feet, and to get out of the shelter system as quickly as possible.

"It's going to take some time for me to save up some money because this job I've got is only minimum wage," I said. "But as soon as I've got first and last month's rent saved up, I'm going to get a place."

"Well, we're not rushing you out the door or anything, here," Andrew said. "If you need to, you can stay here until you turn twenty-two. Because we're a youth shelter, twenty-two is the age limit."

When the intake was over, Andrew showed me around the shelter. Inside, the place was set up like a house. There was a big living room area downstairs with a bunch of couches and a TV. There was a kitchen area. Upstairs, there were bedrooms with bunk beds in them. There was a big shower room with a bunch of shower stalls. There were even washers and dryers on-site, so that you could do your own laundry.

As we walked around, Andrew reminded me of the no-smoking rule. "That door, there, is the door to the balcony," he said. "If you need to have a smoke, you don't have to ask anyone. You can just go outside."

We finished the tour and ended up downstairs in the kitchen area.

"If you're hungry, you can get something to eat," Andrew told me. "All the food is on the table. You just serve yourself here."

"All right," I said. "Thanks."

I went into the kitchen. Everyone had already taken their food and eaten. The TV was on in the living room and they were all in there now, watching some TV show.

I grabbed a plate and went over to the table where all the food was. All kinds of food was set out on different plates, all over the table.

I noticed a few boxes of pizza. I opened one of them. There was still half a pizza in it.

As I was grabbing a slice, someone came into the kitchen. It was one of the guys who was staying at the shelter. He'd obviously just come in from outside because he still had his jacket on.

"Cool," the guy said. "Pizza."

I took two slices and left the box open.

The guy looked at what was left. "Ah, it's got mushrooms on it?" he said.

"You don't like mushrooms?" I said.

"No, I fucking hate them."

The guy checked the other two boxes. They turned out to be empty as well, so he grabbed a slice with mushrooms on it. He picked off all the mushrooms, threw them onto his plate, and then started eating.

As the guy ate, he looked at me. "I've never seen you here before," he said. "You new?"

"Yeah," I said. "I just got here about an hour ago."

The guy nodded as he chewed.

"I'm surprised there's pizza here," I said.

"Yeah, somebody donated it," the guy said. "The shelter gets a lot of donations. Usually, it's pizza. Sometimes it's something else."

"Do they always leave the food out, here?"

"Yeah. No matter what time you come back here at night, you can always get something to eat. You get fed pretty well here."

The guy grabbed another slice of pizza. He picked off all the mushrooms on it, ate it really quickly, and then put his plate on the counter with the rest of the dirty ones.

Right before the guy left the room, he turned to me. "I'm Russ, by the way," he said.

"Jim," I said.

Russ left the kitchen. I finished eating my food, put my plate on the counter, and then went onto the balcony to have a smoke.

The balcony was at the back of the shelter. It was completely enclosed, with a roof overtop of it. It was more of a patio, really, because it was on the ground floor. Also, it was really big. This thing was so big that probably thirty or forty guys could fit onto it all at once. All around the balcony were about as many wooden benches. They were built right into the balcony itself.

There were a couple of guys out on the balcony when I got out there. I didn't talk to them. I just had my smoke and went back inside.

As soon as I got inside, I went into the living room area. Everyone in the room looked at least eighteen years old. Everyone was also male. It was a male-only shelter.

I sat down on one of the couches. I didn't interact with anybody. I just watched the show and kept to myself. I felt out of my element. I was just trying to lay low and check the place out.

At ten o'clock, it was lights out. A few minutes before ten, we all went upstairs and got into our beds. I got a top bunk.

I was glad to get a top bunk. It made me feel secure. Someone couldn't just jump on me if I was on the top bunk. Even if someone tried to grab my arm and pull me down, I wasn't just coming out of there because there was a bar there. I had a chance to grab onto something and react. Turning Point seemed a lot safer to me than the shelter I'd stayed at in Alabama, but at the end of the day, it was still a shelter. I didn't feel like I could really put my guard down.

3

At a quarter to seven the next morning the staff woke everybody up. There was a knock at the bedroom door. "Breakfast in five minutes," a voice said.

I got out of bed and went downstairs with all the other guys. In the kitchen, food was set out on the table like the dinner had been, and you just served yourself. It was like a continental breakfast. They had stuff there like fruit, cereal, bagels, and a whole bunch of scrambled eggs made up on a plate.

I took a plate and put two pieces of toast on it and some scrambled eggs. I usually skipped breakfast in the morning, but I figured I'd better eat. I didn't know when my next meal was going to be.

I felt a little sick as I ate the food, but I forced it down. After I ate, I had a smoke out on the balcony. Then I took a quick shower.

I went back downstairs and hung out in the living room area. At eight o'clock, the staff told everyone that it was time to leave.

Before I left, I got a bag lunch. There was one for everyone staying at the shelter. All the lunches were set out on a table. People were grabbing them, on their way out the door.

My shift at the clothing store didn't start until ten o'clock, so I had some time to kill. I walked to Yonge and Dundas, and then I walked around the general area around the Eaton Centre. At a quarter after nine, I went inside the mall. None of the stores were open yet, but you could go inside and walk around.

I went in through the Queen Street entrance, and then took the escalator downstairs. At the bottom of the escalator was Garage USA. It was an average-sized store. Since it was near the food court, I just sat at a table in the food court and watched the store until somebody showed up there.

At around nine thirty, someone came to open up the store. The guy had a coffee in his hand. He set it down on the ground and then went to unlock the metal security gate at the front of the store.

I walked up to the guy, as he was unlocking the gate. "I'm Jim," I said. "I was hired yesterday to work here as a salesclerk."

The guy shook my hand. "Nice to meet you," he said. "I was told you'd be starting today. My name's Tony. I'm the store manager."

I helped Tony pull back the security gate. We went into the store.

"I'll show you where you can put your stuff," Tony said.

Tony led me to a little room at the back of the store. He showed me to a small locker. "There's no lock on the locker, but your stuff will be safe here," he said. "Nobody comes back here except me and the other salesclerks."

I put my lunch and my jacket into the locker, and then closed it.

Tony handed me my time card. "You can punch in right now," he said.

I punched in.

We left the back room and went back into the store.

"I was told by the general manager yesterday that there's an opportunity to earn a commission here," I said.

"That's right," Tony said. "On big ticket items."

"What's a big ticket item here?"

"Anything leather."

A small section of the store only had leather merchandise in it. It was mainly leather jackets and vests. The rest of the store was pants and shirts. The pants were mainly jeans.

"Leather is our most expensive item," Tony said. "You get fifteen percent commission if you sell leather. If you sell jeans or shirts, you'll get the hourly wage. We're not pressuring you to sell a lot of leather or anything. Most of what we have here is jeans and shirts. The commission is just an incentive."

We walked over to the till.

"I'll show you how to work the cash," Tony said.

In about five minutes, Tony taught me the basics at the cash register.

"Got it," I said.

"You sure?" Tony said. "I can show you again."

"No, that's all right. I'm a pretty fast learner, Tony. All

you have to do is show me one time how to do something and that's all you'll ever have to show me."

Tony smiled. "Good," he said. "Don't worry about returns and stuff like that for now, OK? I'll help you with that when that comes up."

Tony glanced at his watch. "We've got about fifteen minutes before the store opens," he said. "I've got some stock that I need to put out on the floor. Do you mind giving me a hand?"

The stock was in a cardboard box in the back room. Tony brought the box to the front of the store and opened it. It was full of long-sleeve shirts and sweaters.

Tony wanted the shirts folded a certain way. He folded one shirt to show me how to do it. "OK, now you try," he said.

I picked up a shirt and folded it quickly.

"Good," Tony said.

We began folding all of the clothes from the box and stacking them onto a long, rectangular table.

When we were done, Tony looked at his watch. "All right, it's about ten o'clock now," he said. "When customers come into the store, offer to assist them, OK? If they say that they just want to browse, stay nearby. If it isn't busy, you can just straighten the clothes on the racks and re-fold any clothes that customers have looked at. I'll also be on the floor, selling, so it'll be the two of us out here this morning."

Even though I'd never worked in a clothing store before, I was confident that I'd have no trouble selling anything in the store. With clothing, it was easy. If the customer had any questions, you could always read the tag on the clothes.

At the end of Tony's little spiel, he commented on what I was wearing. "By the way, I was told about your situation— how you were stranded in Alabama and all that," he said. "You're dressed all right for today, but we'll figure something out for you in the next couple of days, in terms of clothes."

A few minutes after ten, the first customer walked into the store. It was a guy in his early twenties. He went to look at a pair of jeans.

Tony and I were standing about the same distance from this guy, at opposite sides of the store. I wasn't interested in assisting him, though, because I knew that I couldn't make a commission off jeans.

Tony went and assisted the customer.

A few minutes later, another customer walked into the store. It was some broad in her early twenties. She went straight to the leather section and started to look at a short, bomber-style jacket.

Since Tony was busy, I immediately went over to the leather section to assist the customer. The first thing I did when I got over there was have her try on the coat.

"Why don't you take a look in the mirror?" I said.

All around the store were these full-length mirrors. I'd noticed them when I'd walked into the store with Tony.

I brought the customer over to one of the mirrors. For a few seconds, she looked at herself.

"What do you think?" I said.

"I don't know," the customer said.

"Hold on. Let me fix the collar for you."

I quickly straightened the collar on the jacket. Then I took a step back.

"Yeah," I said, nodding. "That coat really suits you."

"You think so?" the customer said. "I was thinking about getting the brown one."

I wanted to close the sale quickly. I didn't want this broad to start trying on all these fucking coats.

"No, the black one's better," I said. "You know what they say about black—it goes with everything."

The customer laughed. "Yeah, that's true," she said. "All right. I'll take it."

In a couple of minutes, I'd already made one big ticket sale. I glanced over at Tony. He was still helping the guy choose a pair of jeans.

Shortly after I made my first sale, another customer walked into the store. After that, the store was consistently busy. In a couple of hours, I sold another big ticket item.

At around noon, I went on my first break.

"Take fifteen minutes," Tony told me.

I took the escalator to the upper level of the mall and went out through the Queen Street entrance. I stood outside and had a smoke, and then went back to the store.

When I got back, Tony was in the leather section, assisting a customer. "This coat is one hundred percent real lambskin," I heard him say to the guy.

I stood nearby and listened to the rest of Tony's sales pitch. After talking about the material, Tony told the guy how to care for the jacket and clean it. He blabbed so much about the product that it took him ten minutes to make the sale.

I didn't know what the hell I was selling and I'd already sold two jackets. I had no idea if I was selling lambskin, rawhide, or if the shit was even real leather. I didn't know and it didn't seem to matter.

While Tony was at the till with the customer, ringing up

the item, another customer walked in—some guy, wearing work boots. He went straight to the leather section and started eyeing a leather vest.

It literally took me ten seconds to sell the vest to this guy. I just had him try the thing on and look at himself in the mirror, as I stood behind him, straightening the collar.

"Yeah, that's it," I said, as the guy checked himself out. "That looks good, man."

"OK," the guy said. "I'll take it."

At around two o'clock in the afternoon, I went on my half-hour lunch break. I took my bag lunch to the food court, found an empty table, and sat down.

I opened the brown paper bag. Inside, was a baloney and cheese sandwich on white bread, a banana, a granola bar, and a juice box. I ate the food, went outside for a smoke, and then went back to the store.

The store was busy throughout the afternoon. I sold some more big ticket items. My selling technique of having the customer try on the clothes and then look in the mirror turned out to be really effective. It was a big part of making the sale, I realized, having the customer physically put the clothes on their body. Tony just talked the customer's ear off. It didn't matter what he was selling—leather or jeans. It took him ten minutes on average to make one sale. My technique took about ten seconds. It was faster and it enabled me to make a lot more sales.

At six o'clock, my shift was over. In all, I'd sold seven big ticket items. I knew I'd definitely out-grossed Tony. He'd sold mostly jeans and shirts. I knew this because I'd paid attention every time he'd gone to the till. A salesgirl had come into the store in the afternoon. I hadn't seen her sell anything in the leather section.

After I'd punched out and I'd gotten my coat from my locker, Tony called me into his office in the back room. He wanted me to fill out some tax forms. There were two of them. One was provincial, the other was federal.

I started to fill out the first form. When I got to the section that asked for my address, I wasn't sure what to put down. "Should I put the name of the shelter I'm staying at?" I said. "I don't remember the exact street address. I just know it's on Wellesley."

"You can just leave that blank for now," Tony said. "We can update that information when you find a place to live."

I completed the forms and gave them back to Tony.

"When am I going to get my first paycheque?" I said.

"It won't be until the end of November," Tony said. He looked at the calendar on his desk. "November the twenty-ninth. We hold your first paycheque."

I was used to the carnival, where I got paid at the end of every spot.

Oh, well, I thought. At least I know I've got money coming in.

4

I did really well at the clothing store the next day. I sold a lot of big ticket items.

On my third day there, as soon as I came in to work in the morning, Tony had one of the salesgirls hook me up with some clothes. "Dress him in whatever appeals to you," he told the salesgirl.

The salesgirl and I went over to the men's section of the store. She picked out some pants, shirts, and ties for me, and then had me try them on.

In the fitting room, I looked at myself in the mirror. The clothes looked good on me, I thought, even with the running shoes I had on. My shoes were black and plain-looking, though, so they went with anything. I always bought normal-looking shoes. I never bought flashy shit.

I walked out of the fitting room. The salesgirl did the tie up for me. Then she looked me over. "Yeah, that looks good," she said. "I really like that colour on you."

It felt good, having this girl pick out clothes for me. It felt like I was being pampered.

The salesgirl picked out a total of three outfits for me. I wore one and then put the other two sets of clothes in my locker.

I had no idea if Tony was going to charge me for the clothes by deducting them off my paycheque, but I didn't ask him because I figured, what difference did it make? I needed the clothes. I wasn't going to get paid for a while. Tony knew I was in a bad spot and he was just trying to help me out.

While I was at my locker, Tony came over to me. "You're doing a great job, here, Jim," he said. "I'd like you to approach the customers a little more, though, when they walk into the store. If someone comes in and they start looking at jeans or a shirt, offer to assist them. Don't always wait for them to come to you."

I knew what Tony was getting at—he didn't like the fact that I was only paying attention to customers who wanted leather. He was selling everything in the store and so were the two salesgirls. I was consistently out-grossing them all, though, because I was mainly selling stuff in the leather section. I wasn't selling many jeans or shirts.

"OK, I'll make sure to do that," I told Tony.

I had no intention of doing this, though. For the rest of the day, whenever a customer came into the store who wasn't interested in leather, I pretended like I was coming towards the person, but what I did was walk really slowly. There were three salesclerks in the store that day, including myself and Tony, so someone else always got to the customer before I did. At least I'd made the attempt, though, which seemed to please Tony. He never said anything to me about it.

That night, after work, I walked around downtown for about an hour. Then I went back to the shelter.

At around eight o'clock, when most people were back at the shelter for the night, the staff handed out personal needs allowances to everyone. "PNA," they called it. It was twenty-one dollars a week that you could collect every week, apparently.

The PNAs were handed out at the office window to people, one at a time. I waited for my name to be called and then went up to the window. The guy who'd admitted me, Andrew, had me sign for the money. Then he handed me an envelope, containing the cash.

I threw the envelope away and put the cash in my pocket. I already knew how I was going to spend it. I was going to go buy some weed.

I usually smoked weed daily. I hadn't smoked any, though, since before I'd gotten stranded in Alabama. Since I was getting free meals from the shelter, and since I was bumming my smokes, I decided that I could spend the money on weed.

The next day after work, I left the Eaton Centre and walked up Yonge Street. I already knew where I could probably get weed. On the east side of Yonge, south of Gerrard, was this place called the Evergreen. I'd seen it walking to and from work over the previous few days. It was some kind of centre run by the Yonge Street Mission. It was the second building from the corner, on the same block as Sam the Record Man.

To me, the Evergreen was an obvious drug spot. I could tell just by looking at it. There were a couple of guys who looked like drug dealers, hanging out front. They were standing off to the side, in this little corner. The top half of the building was level with the rest of the buildings on the block, but the bottom half, where the door was to go in, was sunk back a few feet from the sidewalk. That was where these guys were hanging out—to the side of the door, in that corner.

There were three dealers hanging out in front of the Evergreen that day. They were all white guys, probably around fifteen to seventeen years old.

I went up to one of the dealers. "Hey, what kind of dope can I get here?" I said.

"Just weed," the guy said. "Nobody sells anything but weed here. If someone tries to do that, they get knocked the fuck out."

"All right. That's what I'm looking for anyway."

"OK. How much do you want?"

"I've got twenty bucks."

I handed the dealer the money. The dealer reached into his pocket and gave me two dime bags.

I put the dimes in my pocket. Then I left the Evergreen and continued walking north on Yonge Street . . .

5

Once I'd settled into the job, the days just went by. Before I knew it, it was the end of November and I was finally getting paid.

The twenty-ninth of November was a Friday. I was scheduled to work that day. At the end of my shift, after I'd punched out, Tony gave me my cheque.

It was essentially two paycheques that I was getting because the store had held my first one. It was a decent-sized paycheque because I'd always made the commission there. I'd never made the minimum wage.

As I left the store that day, I looked at my paystub. I was surprised, when I looked at the deductions, that the store had never charged me for those three sets of clothes they'd given me.

I didn't have a bank account, so the first thing I did when I left the Eaton Centre was go to a cheque-cashing place on

Yonge Street to cash my paycheque. As soon as I did that, I immediately walked over to the Evergreen and bought a couple dimes of weed.

That weekend, I spent a big chunk of my money at Foot Locker in the Eaton Centre. I went in there and bought all these Adidas clothes. I also went to a luggage store in the mall and bought a duffle bag, since I didn't have any luggage.

Even though my plan, when I'd first arrived in Toronto, had been to get the hell out of the shelter system, I was finding it all right staying at Turning Point. I had no rent to pay. I got free meals there. I really was in no rush to leave. I was being given an opportunity, I realized, to get back on my feet. It would have been stupid of me to leave, and then to have to pay rent somewhere else and not be able to buy things I really needed, like clothes.

On Monday morning, when I came in to work, Tony came over to me in the back room, as I was punching in.

"Hey, Jim," Tony said.

"Hey, Tony, what's up?" I said.

"This is going to sound kind of odd, but today, I don't want you to sell anything, OK? I just want you to stand at the front of the store and do security."

Yeah, that does sound odd, I thought.

It was the first week of December now. The Christmas shopping season was in full swing. I was the store's top salesman and my manager was suddenly telling me that he didn't want me to sell anything.

"Tony, what are you talking about?" I said. "It's going to be a huge day today. What do you mean, you don't want me to sell anything?"

"We've got all this merchandise outside the store now,"

Tony said. "Some of it's big ticket stuff. The mall's starting to get really busy with the holiday shoppers. I just want to make sure that nobody steals anything."

We did have a lot of stock outside the store. It was there, in part, to attract customers, but also because we had nowhere else to put it. The store had loaded up on so much merchandise for the Christmas shopping season that stock was literally overflowing from the store.

"Can't you ask one of the salesgirls to do that?" I said.

"I could," Tony said. "But I think it's better if a guy stands out there. Do you know what I mean?"

"OK. Well, what would you be paying me to stand there?

"Six eighty-five an hour."

"*Minimum* wage? Tony, come on. I've never made the minimum wage the whole time I've worked here. It's Christmastime. I'm used to earning a commission. You literally expect me to stand around, of all times of the year, and make minimum wage?"

I could see what was really going on, though. Every day, since I'd started working at Garage USA, I'd out-grossed all of the other salesclerks, including Tony. I'd no sooner gotten my first paycheque and he was demoting me to a security guard position. It wasn't exactly rocket science. The guy just wanted to out-gross me. The only way for him to do it was to have me literally stand there and not sell anything. I wasn't going for it.

"Look, Tony," I said. "I wasn't hired to be a security guard. I know we've got stuff outside the store, but standing there to make sure that nobody shoplifts isn't part of my job description. Now, if you still want me to do security, I'm going to go back there right now and I'm going to get my coat. And if I go back there, I'm telling you,

I'm going to walk out of this store and I'm not going to come back."

"You're being unreasonable," Tony said. "I need you to be a team player, here, Jim."

"OK, then. See ya."

I walked to the back of the store, got my coat out of my locker, and then walked right out of the store.

"You're just going to leave?" Tony said. "That's very unprofessional of you, Jim."

I didn't even look back.

Fuck that job, I thought, as I walked away. I'll just get another sales job somewhere else in the mall.

I walked through the Eaton Centre and immediately tried to find another sales job. I was pretty confident that, with my sales experience, I'd find another job somewhere.

As I walked through the lower level of the mall, I didn't see any "help wanted" signs in any store windows. I decided to just walk into the first decent-looking store I found and talk to the manager.

I quickly found a store that sold men's suits. It was all high-end clothes, so I figured it was a place where you could earn a commission.

I went in and talked to the manager.

"Sorry, but we can't take on any more staff right now," the manager told me. "We hired all of our Christmas help over a month ago. Right now, we're actually overstaffed."

I felt really let down. "OK," I said. "Thanks anyway."

I hit up a bunch of other stores in the mall, but I was told the exact same thing.

That night, when I got back to the shelter, I told the staff that I'd lost my job. I didn't go into specifics with them, and they didn't ask.

"I'm sorry to hear that, Jim," Andrew told me. "You can collect the PNA until you find another job."

6

The next morning, when I woke up, I decided to take another stab at finding work. I left the shelter at eight o'clock and hit up some stores on Yonge Street. That didn't pan out, so I went looking on Queen Street. At every store, however, I got the same result—no one was hiring. "Check back in January," I was told over and over again.

As I was walking around downtown that afternoon, feeling all depressed, I came across a fast food joint that was looking for a fry cook. For a second, I actually thought about walking in there and applying for the job. I'd worked in a food trap on the carnival. I had some experience in fast food.

But a burger joint? I thought. Really?

As desperate as I felt, I didn't want to work for minimum wage. It would have been easier, and just as degrading, to go back to Garage USA and beg Tony to give me the security guard job. At least, there, I'd only have to stand around, watching the store. At Harvey's, I'd have to work my ass off, sweating over a hot grill, for the same crap money. It just didn't make sense to take a job like that.

I decided to pass on the fast food place.

You just need to keep looking, I told myself.

By the end of the day, I still hadn't found anything. I decided to call it quits with the job search. I figured it was pointless. There just weren't any sales jobs around. When the holidays were over and the stores got rid of all their Christmas help, I'd look again, I told myself.

Within a couple of days, being unemployed really started to get to me. The worst part, I found, was the boredom. I had absolutely nothing to do after leaving the shelter at eight o'clock in the morning until I was allowed back there at night. If it was cold, I walked through the malls. There were two other malls near Yonge and Dundas, besides the Eaton Centre. One was the Atrium. The other was a little shopping mall on the east side of Yonge, north of Dundas. There was nothing more depressing than being in a mall, though, a few weeks before Christmas, when you had no money and everyone around you was shopping. After a while, it also got pretty boring, being in the malls.

One afternoon while I was out walking around downtown, feeling bored, I decided to drop by the Evergreen. The whole time I'd worked at the clothing store, I'd heard guys at the shelter saying to each other all the time in the mornings, "I'll see you later, at the Evergreen." I'd bought weed in front of the place with my PNA, but I'd never actually gone inside—not even on my days off. Since I had nothing to do, I decided to go check it out.

I got to the Evergreen at around two o'clock that day. To

get into this place, I learned, you had to go in through two separate doors. Inside the first door was a staircase leading down to a lower level, and an area where people could sit and hang out. Someone who worked at the Evergreen was sitting in this area. She was guarding the second door.

A guy who'd walked in right before I did got stopped at the door. "Could I please see some ID?" the broad said to the guy.

"Yeah, hold on," the guy said.

As the guy reached for his wallet, I looked over at the broad. She smiled at me and nodded. I was obviously the right age to be at the Evergreen. I opened the second door, and then I just walked right in.

Inside this place, it was all big and open. At the very back of the room was a kitchen area. There was a big counter with people standing behind it, serving food.

I went right to the back, where the food was being served. I'd already eaten my bag lunch from the shelter, but I was still kind of hungry. I wanted to have something more to eat.

I went up to the counter. There was a middle-aged broad behind the counter, ladling soup.

"Is this food free?" I said.

"Cold food is free," the broad said. "Hot food is five cents."

The cold food was stuff like bagels and donuts. The hot food was soup and spaghetti. It was cold outside, so I wanted to get something hot. The spaghetti looked like sauce straight out of a can with some noodles, so I decided to get the soup.

"Yeah, can I get some soup?" I said.

The broad picked up a bowl and scooped some soup into

it for me. She glanced up at me. "Have you been here before?" she said. "I don't think we've met."

"No, this is my first time here," I said.

"Well, I'm Karen."

"Jim."

"Nice to meet you, Jim. If you have any questions about the Evergreen, or about any of the services here, feel free to ask me, OK? I'm one of the full-time staff, here. I'm usually here, in the back, serving food."

Karen put my bowl of soup down on the counter. I gave her five cents.

"Enjoy," Karen said.

I picked up my bowl, got a spoon and walked away from the counter. Near the area where the food was served were a bunch of randomly-put round tables. I found an empty one and sat down.

The soup wasn't too great, I realized. There wasn't much to "enjoy" about it. It was probably the blandest soup I'd ever had. It tasted like it was supposed to have two cups of water added to it, but the person who'd made it had added four cups instead.

What do you expect for five cents? I thought. At least it's something warm to eat.

As I sat there, eating, I looked around the room. There were people at other tables, hanging out, eating and talking. It was nothing like Turning Point in terms of the age range. The people here were in their early teens all the way up to probably about twenty-one years old. And it was both genders. It was a place where street-involved youth of all ages, basically, went to hang out and mingle—kind of like a bar, minus the booze.

The atmosphere here was pretty laidback. I just sat at

my table and nobody bothered me. I listened to bits and pieces of other people's conversations, as I ate. It seemed to me like people pretty much respected the place. I didn't see anyone get into an argument or say anything rude to the staff.

Suddenly, some guy came over to my table. "Hey, can I sit here?" he said.

I looked up. This guy was a lot younger than I was. He looked about seventeen years old. He was wearing a Tommy Hilfiger sweater, but it didn't look clean. It looked like he had a mustard stain on it or something.

"Yeah, go ahead," I said.

The guy sat down. He had a bowl of spaghetti.

For a couple of minutes, the two of us just sat there eating and not saying anything. It was kind of uncomfortable, sitting there like this, so I tried to make some conversation.

"Man, I thought the soup would be better than the spaghetti, but it's pretty bad," I said.

"Yeah, I don't like the soup much, here, either," the guy said. "It's too watered down. That's why I got the spaghetti. I don't know why I'm even eating it, though. I'm not even hungry. I had Tim Hortons twice already today."

The guy went on to tell me that he was a panhandler. Some random people had brought him food from Tim Hortons that morning, apparently.

"I do pretty well," the guy said.

"What, with panhandling?" I said.

"Yeah."

The guy leaned over in his chair. He picked up a backpack from off the ground, by his feet. The thing was so full, it was bulging.

"You see this backpack?" the guy said.

"Yeah," I said.

"It's full of all the stuff I got from people this morning."

The guy unzipped the bag and let me see what was in it. He had granola bars in there, sandwiches, a couple of those little oranges, shampoos, tuques, mitts—you name it.

"And this is only the stuff that I kept," the guy said. "Even this bag was given to me. I got it yesterday. It came with a bunch of stuff in it. I get so much stuff on the street everyday that I can't keep all of it. I just keep what I want and give the rest away. You wouldn't believe how much stuff you get panning in this city, man, especially around Christmastime. You get so much shit that you don't even know what to do with it."

As the guy bragged to me about how much free stuff he got panhandling, I couldn't imagine sitting on a street corner like that, asking for handouts. This guy was younger than I was and he seemed perfectly content to be a bum; to sit on his ass all day and get by on donations. I understood old bums that had to do this. They were old. They were all fucked up on booze and drugs. But a young person? A young person should be doing something with himself, I thought. I *wanted* to work. I wanted to earn my money. I didn't want to get by on people's charity. There were obviously a lot of handouts in Toronto, if you knew where to get them, and this panhandler guy was all over that, obviously.

All of a sudden, a bunch of people started heading to the back of the room, where the staff served the food.

The panhandler guy looked at them. "I'll be right back," he said to me. "Watch my food, OK?"

The guy got up and went to the back of the room. A few

seconds later, he came back. He had a couple of Danishes with him.

"They just put these out," the guy said. "That's why everyone was going back there. Just so you know, sometimes the cold food is pretty good, here. If you ever notice lots of people going back there, suddenly, to where they serve the food, it's usually because the staff just put out something good. If you want one of these, by the way, you better go back there quick, before they're all gone."

"It's OK," I said. "I'm good."

The conversation kind of died at this point.

I finished my soup, and then got up from the table. "All right," I said to the guy. "I'll see you around, I guess."

The guy glanced up at me, as he ate one of his Danishes. "Yeah, see ya," he said.

I left the Evergreen. Outside the entrance, a few people were hanging out, smoking cigarettes.

I walked over to where the drug dealers were standing and bought two dimes of weed off one of the dealers. Then I headed over to the park.

Just up the street, on the west side of Yonge, north of Gerrard, was Barbara Ann Scott Park. This park was in behind College Park, which was a big, old building on the southwest corner of Yonge and College, the ground floor of which was a shopping mall. Nearby was the provincial courthouse.

I walked up to the light at Gerrard, crossed, kitty-corner, to the northwest side of the intersection, cut across a big parking lot, and then went right to the back of the park.

In the middle of the park was an oval-shaped skating rink. I sat down near the rink. I took a dime of weed out of my pocket and started to roll a joint.

There weren't many people in the park, so I could do this in plain sight. One person was skating. Two other people were hanging out at the opposite end of the rink from me. From a distance, they looked like college students. Just down the street, off of Gerrard Street East, was the Ryerson College campus.

As I sat in the park, rolling myself a joint, I felt so stressed out about my situation. I was stuck in Toronto, a city that I didn't want to be in, and I was struggling. I knew that once the money I'd made at the clothing store ran out, I'd be living off the personal needs allowance from the shelter until I managed to find another sales job. I wasn't looking forward to it.

I got the joint rolled, lit it up, and took a big toke. I held the smoke in my lungs for as long as I could, and then I exhaled. It was decent weed at the Evergreen. It was kind of orangey-coloured.

Suddenly, I felt the weed high start to come on. I started to mellow out. It really took the edge off, getting high. I always loved that spacey feeling of the marijuana high when it first came on—that feeling of suddenly being high and realizing that you were high. I liked the way smoking weed changed the way I looked at things. I'd notice things in my surroundings that I didn't pay attention to normally, when I wasn't high. I'd have these insights. It was almost like looking at the world through a different pair of eyes.

As I was sitting in this park, getting stoned, I tried to pretend that I wasn't in a big city. There were all these trees around me. They were really tall. You could see them from the southeast corner of Yonge and Gerrard. As long as I didn't look up, and I just looked straight ahead, I didn't really see the buildings. It was easy to pretend that I was somewhere other than downtown Toronto. It was a nice feeling.

After sitting by the skating rink for a while, I started to feel cold.

I decided to get up and go for a walk . . .

7

One morning, about a week after I'd quit my job, I ran into Russ at the shelter. I'd been running into the guy here and there, usually in the kitchen area, ever since that first night at Turning Point, when I'd met him.

Normally, after breakfast, I'd go grab a shower, but because I'd decided to skip one on this particular day—I wasn't working, so I figured, why bother?—I kept talking to Russ and we ended up leaving the shelter together.

As soon as we got out onto the street, Russ asked me if I wanted to go get a coffee.

"Yeah, sure," I said.

"OK, let's go over to Second Cup," Russ said.

The Second Cup coffee store was up the street from the Evergreen. It was on the east side of Yonge, in between Carlton and Gerrard. I'd passed this place lots of times, walking along Yonge, but I'd never gone there to get a coffee. I'd actually never been to a Second Cup anytime I'd ever been in Toronto.

Russ and I walked into the coffee shop. There was a big line in there because it was the morning.

As we stood in the line, I looked around. Right away, I noticed that there was something off about the place. There were a lot of gay people hanging out there, I noticed—way more than you'd expect to find, considering they weren't a huge part of the general population.

Once we'd gotten our coffees, and we were back on the street, I cracked something about this to Russ.

"Yeah, that's Second Cup for you," Russ said.

"I thought it had something to do with it being near the gay neighbourhood," I said.

Turning Point, which wasn't too far from Second Cup, was in a gay neighbourhood. I hadn't realized it the first time I'd gone there because it had been dark outside, but every time I walked down Wellesley Street after that, I noticed that I always saw dykes and fags.

"You mean Church and Wellesley?" Russ said.

"Yeah," I said.

"No, it has nothing to do with that. They're all like that— all the Second Cups in Toronto. It's just a gay fucking coffee store. No matter which one you go to in this city, you'll always find at least one or two homos hanging out in the place. The only reason I go to this one is because it's close to the Evergreen. I used to go there all the time, when I was younger. This was the nearby hangout. You know what we used to call this place?"

"What?" I said.

"*Suction* Cup."

I laughed.

"That's a good one, eh?" Russ said.

"Yeah," I said. "It is."

Right outside the coffee shop was a patio that was closed for the season. Right off the patio was a footpath.

Russ went onto the path. "Come on," he said. "Let's go to the park."

Russ and I walked along the path to the park. It was a very small park. Joseph Sheard Parkette, it was called. It was just a small grassy area with some trees and a few benches. It was hidden away from the main street, behind the buildings. It was kind of private back there.

Russ and I sat down on one of the benches.

"Want to smoke a joint?" Russ said.

"Sure," I said.

Like me, Russ was obviously a pothead. It was only the morning and he wanted to smoke up.

Russ already had a joint rolled. He lit it up and took a big haul. Then he passed it to me.

As we sat there, talking and passing the joint back and forth, Russ told me more about the Evergreen.

"I still go there sometimes, like if I've got nothing to do during the day and I'm bored, but not too often, really," Russ said. "These days, it's more like once in a while. For the longest time, though, I went there all the time and bought my weed there. It's a well-known place to buy weed. Even tourists know this."

"Yeah, that's where I've been going to buy weed," I said.

"It's such a rip-off buying it there, though. Those guys never give you proper counts. You're getting like half a gram for ten bucks. I can get you weed, Jim, if you want. I know a guy who'll give you a way better deal."

Because I was buying such small quantities of weed, I

told Russ not to bother. I only bought small amounts because I didn't want to take much weed with me back to the shelter at night. Every day I was buying one or two dimes. I'd get two joints out of a dime.

"That's cool," Russ said. "Just let me know if you change your mind. I can get you weed. I can get you anything you want in terms of drugs."

We hung out for a while longer. Then Russ told me that he had to go do some stuff. He didn't say what he had to do exactly, and I didn't ask. I figured if Russ had wanted to tell me, he would have told me. I just assumed he had some kind of hustles going on.

Russ and I left the park. When we got back onto Yonge Street, we went our separate ways.

"Have a good one," Russ said.

"Yeah, you, too," I said.

For a while, I walked around. I went to different places—College Park, the Atrium, and the Eaton Centre.

Later that day, in the afternoon, I went to the Evergreen. I'd been going there ever since that first day I'd gone there to check the place out. It killed time, I found, and it helped break up the afternoon.

That day, while I was at the Evergreen, I overheard some guy talking about his GST cheque. He was sitting at the table next to mine, telling some guy about how he had to go to his mom's house somewhere in Toronto the next day to pick it up.

I hadn't done my taxes in three years. Hearing this got me thinking. If I filed a return for those three years, I knew I'd get a lot of money back—three years of GST, plus whatever I got back from doing my taxes because I'd gone in the books that whole time on the show and my income had been taxed. The only problem was, unlike this guy, I didn't have a mom living nearby, whose address I could use to get mail. I could file a return, but where would the government send the cheque? I was staying in a shelter. I had no mailing address.

I didn't even know if this guy who'd been talking about his GST even lived with his mom at all, or if he just had his mail going to her place. What I'd learned from hanging out at the Evergreen, and from overhearing people's conversations there, was that not everyone who hung out there was homeless. Some people just went there during the day to hang out. At night, they went home to their parents.

That night, when I got back to the shelter, I ran into Russ. We had something to eat, and then we went out onto the balcony to have a smoke.

There were some people out on the balcony, so we went to the far side, away from everyone else. We hung out there for a little while and just talked and smoked.

I decided to tell Russ about my tax problem. I felt I could trust him enough. It was obvious that the guy had been on the street for a while. I was wondering if he could give me some advice.

"The problem is that I don't have a mailing address," I said to Russ. "I don't want to use Turning Point as my address because then they'll know I'm getting this money."

"There's an easy way around that," Russ said.

"Yeah, what?"

"Get a P.O. Box. That's what I use to get mail. I don't have anything going to fucking Turning Point."

"How much do they cost?"

"They're about ten bucks a month."

I suddenly realized that I didn't even know where to go in Toronto to get my T4 slips.

"I'll tell you what," Russ said. "I've got to go check my mail tomorrow morning. Why don't you come with me to the post office? You can get a P.O. Box, and then I'll show you where to get your T4s."

"Thanks," I said. "I really appreciate it, man."

"No problem," Russ said.

The next morning, Russ and I left the shelter and walked to a Canada Post outlet not far from the Evergreen. While Russ checked his mail, I got in the line to go up to the counter.

The line wasn't too long. It moved quickly. Within a few minutes, I was at the counter, talking to the clerk.

Luckily, there was a postal box available for me at the location we were at. "You'll just need to fill out this form, here, and then pay the fee," the clerk said.

I filled out the form and then paid the fee, which included the refundable deposit for the keys. You could rent the box for three, six, or twelve months at a time, so I went with three months.

The clerk assigned me a P.O. Box, and then gave me the keys for it.

Russ was waiting for me at the back of the line. "Everything go OK?" he said.

"Yeah," I said.

I told Russ my box number.

"Hey, I'm only four boxes down from you," Russ said.

Russ and I left the post office. He brought me over to the Revenue Canada tax services office. The place was on Front Street, in between Bay and Yonge.

Russ had to go do some stuff when we got to Revenue

Canada, so I told him that I'd see him later, and then went inside the building. There was a lineup. I got into the line.

When I finally got up to the counter, I told the clerk that I wanted my T4s.

"Yes, I can help you with that," the clerk said. "First, I'll just need your social insurance number, so I can look you up in our system."

I gave the clerk my SIN number.

"Perfect," the clerk said. "And could I please have two pieces of government-issued ID?"

I gave the clerk two pieces of ID.

"Thank you," the clerk said. She looked at the IDs, and then handed them back to me.

"It's been three years since I did my taxes," I said.

The clerk was looking at her computer screen. "Yes, I see that, here," she said. "You haven't filed for the following years: 1995, 1994, and 1993."

"That's right. Could I get my T4s for those years?"

"Sure. Is there anything else I can do for you today?"

"No, that's it."

The clerk printed off my T4 slips for me. I took them, left the Revenue Canada office, and then immediately went to an accounting business on Yonge Street that did taxes. I just kept walking from Front Street until I found one.

The accountant did my taxes for me on the spot. I sat in the office and waited. It wasn't a busy time of year for these people, so I was the only customer in there.

When the accountant was finished doing all the paperwork, she had me sign the forms.

"How long will it take for me to get my refund, do you think?" I said.

"About six to eight weeks," the accountant said.

"Do you think I might get it sooner, seeing as how it's not tax time right now?"

"Probably not. That's the standard turnaround time for the tax centre in Sudbury."

"OK," I said.

I was honestly just happy I'd have some money soon.

8

I had nothing to do but wait on my tax refund. Every day the money I'd made at Garage USA just kept dwindling.

One night, I went back to the shelter early, when the shelter staff let everyone in. I did this because I was bored and I had nothing else to do.

I ate dinner with the guys at the shelter. After I'd finished eating, I hung out in the kitchen area, at one of the tables, and talked to people. The whole time I'd worked at the clothing store, I'd never really talked to anyone at the shelter except Russ, when I ran into him. Now that I wasn't working anymore, and I'd been staying there for a while, I felt that it was time to start interacting with other people more. It was getting depressing, never really talking to anyone.

That night, while I was hanging out in the kitchen area, I met this guy who washed car windows at traffic lights every day for spare change. That was how he made his money, he told me. He was a "squeegee kid." In Toronto, that was what people called these guys.

I already knew this guy washed windows because I'd seen him coming and going from the shelter all the time with a squeegee. Most of the people who did this I'd noticed, were punkers and skinheads, but this guy wasn't a punk or anything. He was just a normal-looking guy. He always wore a green hoodie.

While this guy and I were talking, I mentioned at some point during the conversation that I was broke.

"Why don't you come wash windows with me tomorrow morning?" the guy said.

The guy's name was Mark.

"Ah, I don't know, Mark," I said.

I really wasn't interested in squeegeeing. It just didn't appeal to me. It was better than panhandling, I thought, but it wasn't a whole lot better, in my eyes. With squeegeeing, you were really putting yourself out there in a public way that you were hurting; that you'd been reduced to working for nickels and dimes. I was in a bad spot financially, like the rest of these guys on the street, but I couldn't imagine doing something like this. It might have had something to do with the fact that I still had money left from what I'd made at the clothing store. Maybe I just wasn't that desperate yet or something.

I told Mark that I'd pass on the window washing.

"You should give it a try," Mark said. "I'm telling you, you'll make a lot of money."

"Yeah?" I said. "How much are we talking about?"

"Well, you've never done it before, so I don't know exactly what *you'd* make, but every day that I'm out there,

I'm making twenty to twenty-five bucks an hour."

"Wow."

I had no idea these guys made that kind of money. I didn't even think they made half that much.

"Yeah, and it's all tax-free, baby," Mark said. "Name me one job that you can get in Toronto without a high school diploma that's going to pay you that kind of cash."

I still didn't want to do it. If I could make twenty bucks an hour, though, I was willing to at least give it a try. If I didn't like it, I just wouldn't do it again, I thought.

"So, what do you say?" Mark said. "Are you going to come with me tomorrow morning?"

"All right," I said. "Sure. What the hell?"

In the morning Mark and I left the shelter at around seven thirty. We walked over to Church and Bloor, where Mark worked. Church and Bloor was about a ten-minute walk from the shelter. It was only a block east of Yonge Street, so it was a really busy intersection.

As soon as we got to Mark's corner, which was at the northeast side of the intersection, Mark started to tell me where I could go to get a squeegee. "There's a Canadian Tire not far from here, off Church Street," he said. "It opens at eight. It's only about a five-minute walk from here, though, so, . . ."

I didn't even let Mark finish his sentence. Before he could finish telling me how to get to the Canadian Tire, I interrupted him. I'd already lost my nerve to go through with the squeegeeing thing. It had taken a lot for me to even agree to come to the corner with him. Now that I was standing there, looking at the road and at all the cars piling up at the traffic light, I just couldn't bring myself to actually do it.

"You know what?" I said to Mark. "I think I'm just going to check it out first. You don't mind if I just hang out here for a while and watch you work, do you?"

Mark didn't seem to care. "Yeah, that's fine," he said. "Go ahead. I'm going to go inside to get something to eat right now. If you want, you can come with me."

Mark and I went inside the big building on the northeast corner of the intersection. We went to a coffee shop on the ground floor. It wasn't a chain; it looked like a family-owned place.

I followed Mark up to the counter. He made some small talk with the old guy behind the till.

"Hey, how's it going?" the old guy said to Mark.

"Not bad," Mark said. "Can I get a breakfast sandwich and a coffee?"

"Sure," the guy said.

The guy punched some buttons on the cash register. He told Mark the total cost of the food.

Mark reached into his pocket and pulled out a handful of change. He put more money down on the counter than what the food cost. It looked like he gave the guy at least a few extra bucks.

Mark and I stepped aside and let the next person in line go up to the counter. We waited at the end of the counter, while Mark's order got made.

"You're not going to get anything?" Mark said to me, as we were standing there, waiting.

"Nah, I had a donut at the shelter," I said.

I did have a donut at the shelter, but I probably could have eaten some more food. I didn't order anything, though, because I didn't want to spend the money. I was getting low on funds.

In a couple of minutes, Mark's food was ready. Mark took his tray and then we went and found a table.

Mark ate quickly. When he was done, he took his tray back up to the counter. Then he asked the old guy behind the till if he could have a bucket of water.

"Sure," the guy said.

The guy left the counter and went into the back room, where the kitchen was located. He came back a minute later with a five-gallon bucket filled with water. There were no suds in it. It was just plain water.

Mark took the bucket from the guy. "Thanks," he said.

"Have a nice day," the guy said.

The two of us left the coffee shop.

As we headed back outside, Mark explained to me what the deal was with the guy at the coffee shop. "I eat there all the time and give the owner five-dollar tips," he told me. "That's why he gives me a bucket of water every day."

When we got outside, Mark took his bucket right to the corner of Church and Bloor. He put it down at the curb. Then he took his squeegee—he used the kind with the wooden handle—put it in the bucket, and waited for the next red light on Bloor.

At the northeast corner, Mark was getting the cars travelling westbound along Bloor Street.

"This is a good corner because you get the traffic coming off the DVP," Mark said.

"What's that?" I said.

"The DVP?"

"Yeah."

"It's a freeway—the Don Valley Parkway. You're not from Toronto, I take it."

"No, I'm not."

"OK. Well, the Bayview exit off of the Don Valley is about a five-minute drive from here. When the cars come off the highway, the windows are usually dirty. So, it's a good corner."

The light turned red.

Mark pulled his squeegee out of his bucket. He flicked the water off of it a couple of times, so that it wouldn't drip down, onto his glove. Then he held his squeegee up in the air and walked out into the road.

There were two lanes of cars travelling westbound on Bloor Street. Mark walked down the middle, in between the two lanes of westbound cars.

The second car in the lineup had a dirty windshield. Mark approached the car.

The driver waved to Mark, letting him know that it was OK for him to clean his window. Mark didn't just do the windshield. He did that, plus all the other windows on the car.

When Mark was done, the driver rolled down his window and gave Mark some change. Mark put the change in his pocket, and then rung his squeegee out onto the ground. He just gave it a good jerk to get most of the dirty water off of it.

There was still some time left on the light, so Mark went to look for another car. He held up his squeegee again and approached a car with a dirty window. This driver wasn't interested, though. I saw him mouth the word "no" to Mark. He then immediately held up his hand and started shaking his head.

Mark didn't bother with this guy. He just walked further on down the lineup. There was no shortage of cars. There were tons of them, backed up at the light.

Mark found another car. He did the windows really quickly. As the light changed, he came back to the curb.

"How'd you do?" I said.

"Not bad," Mark said. "I made about two and a half bucks."

Mark and I talked for a bit, while he waited for the next red light.

"Usually, they give me a loonie or something," Mark said. "Sometimes they don't have any loonies or toonies on them, so they'll just give me a bunch of change—whatever they've got in their car."

Suddenly, the light changed. Mark pulled his squeegee out of his bucket, flicked the water off of it, and then got back to work.

After about half an hour, Mark took a little break. He didn't go anywhere; he just stood at the corner and skipped the next few red lights.

"All right, I guess it's time to get back to work," Mark said all of a sudden.

"I'm going to take off now," I said.

"Yeah? Already?"

"Yeah. I've got to go do some stuff. I'll see you later, OK?"

"OK. Later, Jim."

As I walked along Bloor Street, towards Yonge Street, I thought about what I'd just seen at Church and Bloor. The whole squeegeeing thing—it didn't really seem too bad, honestly. You were working for spare change, but at least you were *working*. You were providing a service and you were asking people if they wanted it. There was dignity in that. And if you did it for enough hours in the day, it looked like you could actually make some money at it.

9

I decided the next morning that I was going to wash windows. When I got to the corner with Mark, however, I didn't end up doing it. I just hadn't worked up enough nerve yet.

Since I was at the corner already, I hung out with Mark again and watched him work.

Mark didn't mind. "It's actually kind of nice, having somebody to talk to," he told me. "I've always worked by myself here. Most of the guys that do this are French and they all kind of stick together. They come here from Montreal and move around the city in little groups."

I'd seen these French guys hanging out at the Evergreen all the time. I knew they squeegeed because they came in there with their squeegees sticking out of their backpacks. They would hang out together at their own tables and never talk to anyone else. All the time, you'd hear them talking French. They were all hardcore punk rockers, too. They had Mohawks. They had piercings in their faces. They had the anarchy symbol all over their clothes.

The light changed. Mark got to work.

While Mark worked, I paid close attention to what he was doing. I watched him walk down the middle, in between the two lanes of cars, and approach the second car in the lineup—a Mercedes Benz. The guy in the Mercedes didn't want his windows washed. He shook his head and waved Mark away. Mark didn't try to wash the guy's windows. He just put his squeegee back up in the air and went to look for another car.

After watching Mark for a while, I noticed that he didn't really have much of a strategy in terms of what he was doing. All he did, basically, was walk down the middle, in between the cars, and hold out his squeegee. If the driver said yeah, then he did the guy's windows. If the driver said no, then he didn't. That was it. That was pretty much the extent of it.

After hanging out at the corner with Mark for about forty-five minutes, I decided to take off. I could have left to go get a squeegee at this point and then jumped in—I was feeling a little more confident, just watching Mark work— but I decided not to do this. I was still testing the waters, really. I was still asking myself, "Can I do this?"

I thought I'd go back to the corner the next day, but I didn't end up going there. I just didn't feel like it when I got up in the morning. I spent the day, instead, walking around downtown by myself. I hung out in the malls. As usual, it was boring.

I noticed, while I was walking around that day, that whenever I saw some squeegee kids, I'd pay attention to them. There were lots of them in the downtown core. Most of them were in their mid-teens to around mid-twenties. I usually saw them working in pairs. Now that I was actually thinking of squeegeeing, myself, I was taking note of what these guys were doing out on the street.

Most of these guys, I noticed, took the same approach to squeegeeing that Mark did; they just held out their squeegees and walked down the lineup, looking for a driver that would let them clean their windows. But then there were other squeegee kids who were more aggressive. They'd do the person's windows even if the person didn't want them to, and then they'd expect some money for it.

That day, while I was out walking around, I came across these two squeegee kids, working at Bay and Queen, by Old City Hall.

As I stood at the corner, waiting for the light, I watched these two guys walk down the lineup of cars. They were getting cars going westbound on Queen Street. One guy had a huge red Mohawk. The other guy had spikes sticking out of his head about a foot high.

The guy with the spikes went up to the second car in the lineup. It was a new-looking Mustang, a really nice car. The driver clearly didn't want his windows washed. He immediately shook his head and tried to wave the squeegee kid away. The guy didn't pay any attention to him, however. He just took his squeegee and dragged it across the windshield of the guy's car.

When the guy was done washing the windshield, he stuck his hand out at the driver's side window, expecting some money for the work he'd just done. The driver didn't roll down his window, though. He just sat there, looking angry, and staring straight ahead, at the road.

The squeegee kid swore at the driver. Then he went to look for another car.

Soon, the light changed. The two squeegee kids came back to the curb. The Mustang drove off.

As I started to cross the street, I thought to myself about what I'd just seen.

Yeah, no shit the guy didn't want his windows washed, I thought. He's got a decent fucking car.

A lot of these morons, these punks, I'd noticed, wore clothes that had pieces of metal sticking out of them. The guy with the spikes, for instance, had on a jean jacket with a leather vest overtop of it that was covered in metal studs. As soon as this guy got up close to a car to clean the windshield, he was going to scratch it. I could understand why the driver of the Mustang didn't want this kid to touch his car. He didn't want the paint job on his nice, brand new car to get all scratched up. And who the fuck could blame him?

I witnessed some similar incidents as I walked around downtown that day.

By the end of the day, when I got back to the shelter, I was pretty convinced that if I actually tried squeegeeing, I could probably do a lot better than most of these squeegee kids out there. I wasn't some dirty punk with metal studs sticking out of my clothes. I was clean-cut. I was approachable-looking.

I could probably get a lot of these cars *with* their permission, I thought.

10

It took a couple more days, but I finally worked up the nerve to get out there and squeegee. It was five days before Christmas when this happened. I was down to my last twenty bucks. I knew that when the twenty bucks ran out, I'd be living off the PNA from the shelter until I managed to find another sales job, or until I got my tax refund in the mail—whichever came first. Financially, I had no other options.

I ran into Mark that morning at the shelter. We left and walked over to Church and Bloor.

As soon as we got to the corner, I turned to Mark. "Hey, where's that Canadian Tire you were telling me about the other day?" I said. "I want to go there and get a squeegee."

Mark told me where the store was. "It's a couple of blocks north of Bloor, off Church," he said. "It'll be on your right-hand side. You can't miss it. They're not open yet, though, just so you know. They don't open until eight."

It was only seven forty in the morning. It was only going to take me a few minutes to walk over there, so I went to the coffee shop with Mark to kill some time.

Mark got a breakfast sandwich. I didn't get anything because I didn't have enough money.

We sat down at a table. When Mark was done eating, he went to the counter and got his bucket. I immediately headed over to the Canadian Tire.

North of Bloor Street, Church Street headed in a northwestern direction, ending at Yonge Street. Right at the corner of Yonge and Church was a Canadian Tire gas station. Right behind it, was the Canadian Tire store.

I went into the store, and then went to the aisle where they had the squeegees. They had all kinds of different ones. I got the cheap kind with the wooden handle that Mark used.

I left the store and walked back to Church and Bloor. Mark was at the corner, waiting for the next light.

"See, it wasn't too far, eh?" Mark said.

"Yeah, it was about five minutes," I said.

I put my squeegee in the bucket with Mark's.

In about a minute, the light changed. Mark pulled his squeegee out of his bucket. I pulled mine out, too, flicked the water off of it, like I'd seen Mark do, and then I held it up in the air and followed Mark out into the road.

I took the lineup of cars in one lane. Mark took the cars in the other lane, closest to the sidewalk.

Even though I'd observed it a bunch of times, it was still nerve-wracking to actually be doing this. As soon as I stepped into the road, my heart started pounding in my chest. I felt nervous and self-conscious, suddenly. It was the same feeling I'd had the first time I'd ever stepped into a game on the carnival. I knew that once I'd broken the ice and I'd gotten my first customer, everything would be fine, but for those first few seconds, I had a lot of anxiety.

I walked down the lineup and held up my squeegee. I didn't approach just any car, though, like I'd seen Mark do. Instead, I tried to look for a motorist who I thought would let me wash their windows and who'd give me some money for it. Just like on the carnival, I didn't call in every single person who walked by my game. I tried to read people and pick the ones out of the crowd that I thought would spend money—the *live* ones. In this case, I was also looking for a person whose car had at least a semi-dirty windshield. But since these cars had just come off the freeway, most of the windshields were dirty.

The third car in the lineup was a Honda Civic. The driver was a middle-aged broad.

The broad made eye contact with me. She had a neutral expression on her face. She was kind of hard to read. I didn't get a bad vibe from her, though, so I decided to approach her car.

Right away, the broad started to shake her head at me. "No, no, no," she was saying.

Hmm, I thought. If I can get a smile out of this broad, maybe she'll let me do it.

I made a funny gesture. I just did the first thing that popped into my head. I stretched my arms out, held my palms up, and cocked my head to one side. Then I frowned, like I was really sad that the broad didn't want me to clean her windows. I was just trying to act goofy. I just wanted to get a rise out of this person. I just wanted to make her smile.

Immediately, I got a reaction. The broad smiled.

"Don't worry," I said.

I mouthed the words slowly so that the broad could understand what I was saying, since her windows were rolled up and she couldn't hear me.

"It's free," I said. "No money."

The broad nodded. I saw her lips move. "OK," she said.

The car was really dirty. This broad really did need her windows washed. I couldn't even see through the side windows that well. They were covered in a grey film. This film was all over the windows and the body of the car. This was from dirt, grime, and salt. It hadn't snowed yet in Toronto, but it was cold enough that the city had been salting the roads and sidewalks to prevent ice from forming on them. The salt got on everything.

The first thing I did was the windshield. Then I cleaned the driver's side window. After that, I went around to the back of the car, cleaning all the windows. I finished up on the passenger side.

When I got back around to the driver's side window, the broad had her purse in her lap. She took out her change purse, and then rolled down her window. She handed me a loonie and a few nickels and dimes. This was exactly what I'd figured this broad would do. I'd made her smile. I'd offered to wash her windows for free. Now she felt obligated to pay me.

"I'm sorry, but that's all the change I've got on me," the broad said.

"That's all right," I said. "Thanks"

"Have a nice day."

"You, too."

The broad rolled her window back up. I stepped away

from the car and then rang out my squeegee onto the ground. I did what I'd seen Mark do—I gave the thing a good jerk and got most of the dirty water off of it.

It had taken me about a full minute to clean all of the windows on the Honda Civic. I'd gotten a few streaks, but I hadn't done too bad of a job.

I still had some time left on the light, so I looked for another car.

I noticed a guy who was calling me over. He was driving a jeep. The windows were pretty dirty.

I did the windshield and some of the other windows on the jeep. I looked up at the light. It turned yellow, suddenly. I wasn't done yet, but I was out of time.

I hurried over to the driver's side window. The guy already had his window rolled down.

I put my hand out. The guy gave me a toonie. Suddenly, the car in behind beeped.

I put the money in my pocket and then went back to the curb.

While waiting for the next light, I talked to Mark.

"See, it's pretty easy, huh?" Mark said.

"Yeah, it's all right," I said.

"You get fast at it."

"How long have you been doing this?"

"Not that long. Since about mid-October."

Even though I wasn't that fast at it yet, I was pretty good with the squeegee. I wasn't getting a lot of streaks. I knew I could pick up my speed if I just worked at it.

After a few more lights, I started to get a lot faster. The money started to add up in my pocket. I already had more than what I would have made in an hour at a minimum wage job.

After about an hour, I felt like I'd finally gotten the hang of it. One hour in, and it was already like nothing. I wasn't even getting any more streaks.

Mark's right, I thought. This *is* easy.

At around ten o'clock, rush hour ended. Because we were right downtown, on a main drag, there were still a lot of cars on the road.

Mark and I hadn't taken any breaks yet—not even to go take a piss. We decided to take a smoke break.

We let a few lights go by, as we stood at the corner, smoking. Then we got back to work.

I walked into the road and approached the first car in the lineup. The driver shook his head at me and tried to wave me off.

I did my funny gesture. The guy smiled.

OK, I thought. Go ahead.

As soon as I took a step towards the car, however, the driver immediately started shaking his head at me again. He clearly didn't want his windows done.

"Don't worry," I said. "It's free."

The guy was still shaking his head. I decided not to bother with the guy. I just went and looked for another car.

At around noon, Mark and I decided that we were done work for the day.

"I've made enough money," Mark said to me. "I'm ready to get out of here."

I had no idea how much money Mark had made because he hadn't told me. I figured, though, that if he was making twenty to twenty-five bucks an hour on an average day, like he'd told me, then I'd definitely out-grossed him. I'd already made about a hundred and sixty bucks.

I knew the reason I'd done so well, squeegeeing, was

because of my act; how I'd tried to entertain people a little bit. And also because of how I hadn't just been approaching any random car in the lineup. Most of the time, I realized, I could pick the right car. Aside from the one guy who'd waved me off, even after I'd done my silly gesture, everyone else that I'd approached that morning had let me do their windows, and they'd all given me at least one or two bucks for doing them. I'd made good money and I'd never, once, had to be aggressive with anyone. If I could make the person smile, I learned, it was usually smooth sailing.

"I'm going to get out of here, too," I said to Mark.

"OK, let's go dump this water," Mark said.

Mark and I went over to a nearby sewer grate on Church Street. We dumped our water down the grate. Because we'd been ringing out our squeegees on the ground before putting them back into our bucket at the end of each light, the water wasn't even that dirty yet. We could have gone for quite a while longer before we'd had to change it.

Mark had the bucket in his hand. "I'll go bring this back to the coffee shop," he said.

"OK," I said. "I'll wait here."

Mark went inside the building. I had a smoke while I waited for him to come back.

When Mark got back, he told me that he was going to go get a twenty piece of crack from his dealer. "Do you want me to get you some?" he said.

Even though I smoked crack sometimes, I thought it would be a bad idea to smoke it, at least for the time being. I was already on the street. I didn't need to make my situation any worse by using that shit and maybe having it get out of control. I was afraid that if I had Mark run for me, I'd get high, and then I'd fall in and end up spending every last penny I'd made, squeegeeing, on dope.

I told Mark that I wasn't interested. "I'm just sticking to weed right now," I said.

"All right," Mark said. "No problem. I just thought I'd offer. I don't really smoke it much myself, honestly. I'm not like some of these guys out here who literally go get high as soon as they've made twenty bucks. I just feel like using today. I don't know why."

I told Mark that I'd see him later, back at the shelter. Then we went our separate ways.

Since the Evergreen wasn't open yet—the place didn't open until one o'clock—I decided to go to Foot Locker in the Eaton Centre. I wanted to buy some more clothes. I knew that I could make the same money squeegeeing the next day, so I didn't care if I spent a hundred bucks in there.

As I walked through the mall to Foot Locker, I happened to notice some dirt on my pants. It was that grey-coloured shit that had been on all the cars. To do the windshields, I'd had to get really close-up to the cars and that's how that stuff had gotten on my clothes. The next day, I realized, I was going to have to put on my crappy, old pants that I'd had since Alabama overtop of my good ones before going to the corner in the morning to squeegee.

11

Over the next three days, I went to Church and Bloor with Mark every morning and squeegeed. Every day by noon, I managed to make about two hundred bucks.

My fifth day out there was the day before Christmas. That morning, when Mark and I got to our corner, there weren't too many cars on the road.

"I think a lot of people aren't going in to work today," Mark said to me.

"Yeah, no kidding," I said.

The twenty-fifth of December was in the middle of the week. It was a Wednesday. It made sense that a lot of people would take the day before off work.

At first, I thought I wasn't going to make much money. Normally, there were so many cars at the light that I could always find someone whose windows I could wash. Now, there weren't so many.

Let's see how this goes, I thought.

Mark and I went to the coffee shop, ate, got our bucket, and then went to the curb.

The light changed. I pulled my squeegee out of the bucket, flicked the water off of it, and then held it out and walked into the road.

The first car in the lineup called me over. I washed all of the windows and then went to the driver's side. The driver rolled down her window and gave me twenty bucks.

"Wow," I said. "Thanks."

"You're welcome," the broad said. "Merry Christmas."

I walked down the lineup and did another car. This guy gave me a ten-dollar bill.

After that, it was pretty much all tens and twenties. The least someone gave me for doing their windows was a five-dollar bill.

Less than an hour into the workday, this van pulled up, suddenly. The driver waved to me, and then rolled down his window. "Hey," the guy said. "If you can do all the windows on my van by the time this light changes, I'll give you this hundred-dollar bill."

The guy had a bill in his hand. It was a brown one.

"Sure," I said. "I'll do all of your windows, man."

The guy was driving a brand new Dodge Caravan. It was the long kind—the extended model.

I went all around the car and washed all of the windows. When I was done, I had enough time left on the light that I could have done another car. I'd gotten so fast already that I could do all the windows on a minivan in under forty-five seconds. The light at Church and Bloor was ninety seconds long.

The guy gave me the hundred dollars, as promised.

"You're pretty fast," he said.

"Yeah, well, you got to figure, I do this for four hours straight every morning," I said.

The guy laughed. "Gotcha," he said.

At ten o'clock, Mark told me that he was going to take off.

"Yeah?" I said. "You're quitting already?"

The money was so good. It didn't make sense, in my opinion, to leave early.

"Yeah, I've already grabbed about a hundred bucks," Mark said. "I want to go get high."

"All right," I said.

"OK, Jim. I'll see you later."

Mark took off. I went back to work.

Over the next two hours I got a lot more ten- and twenty-dollar bills. I even had another car give me a hundred-dollar bill. By the time noon came around, I was ready to quit for the day. I'd made about four hundred bucks.

I dumped my water, returned the bucket to the coffee shop, and then walked over to the Eaton Centre. The mall was full of people running around, trying to finish their last-minute shopping.

I went downstairs to Foot Locker, blew most of the money I'd made that morning, and then left the mall and walked up Yonge Street to the Evergreen.

I knew all the dealers there by this point.

"Hey, Craig," I said.

"Hey, what's up?" Craig said.

"Can I get two dimes?"

For the rest of the afternoon, I smoked weed and walked around downtown, all stoned.

At six o'clock at night, I decided to go to the shelter. I didn't feel like going back there yet, but because it was Christmas Eve, there was nowhere else to go; all the malls were closed.

There was nothing special going on back at the shelter. The staff had decorated the place, but it was, otherwise, like any other day there.

After dinner, I hung out in the living room and watched Christmas movies on TV. At ten o'clock, it was lights out, as usual. Everyone went to bed.

In the morning, because it was Christmas Day, the staff let everyone stay at the shelter for the entire day. We didn't have to leave by eight o'clock, like we usually did. The staff put Christmas music on. They gave out little gifts to everyone, like socks and whatnot. They even served a turkey dinner. Like all of the meals there, the food was set out on the kitchen table and you just put whatever you wanted onto your plate.

All in all, it wasn't too bad of a day. It was a lot better than hanging out in the street or having to go out and squeegee. The only thing that kind of bothered me about it was when I walked by the pay phone at one point, by the office window, and I overheard someone talking to a relative or something. I'd spent a lot of Christmases without my family since I'd left Edmonton with the carnival, but I think that because I was in a homeless shelter, it kind of got to me. I could have called my mom, but I was still pissed off at her for not helping me in Alabama. As for the rest of my family, I'd lost touch with everyone when I'd left town with the show in July '92. I still had their phone numbers, assuming they hadn't changed, but I didn't think anyone would want to talk to me. I didn't want to call someone and then have the phone slammed down in my ear.

I didn't stew over these depressing thoughts for too long. The next day, Christmas was all over. It was back to work as usual. December the twenty-sixth was Boxing Day in Canada, the biggest shopping day of the year.

I got up in the morning and went to Church and Bloor with Mark to go squeegee. There were tons of cars on the road.

When we finished work at noon that day, Mark wanted to go hang out. "Let's go to a hotel or something," he said. "I don't feel like going back to the shelter tonight."

"OK," I said. "Where do you want to go?"

Mark knew about a cheap hotel on Spadina and College. "It's called the Waverly," he said. "We can get a double room there for about fifty bucks."

Before Mark and I went to the Waverly, we stopped by the Evergreen to get some weed. I got ten dimes because the dealer was willing to give me a deal. I didn't care about having that much weed on me because I wasn't going back to the shelter that night.

After we got our weed, Mark and I hung out in front of the Evergreen for a while. We talked to the drug dealers until the place opened at one o'clock. At that point, we went inside, went straight to the back, where the food counter was, and got a hot meal, each, for five cents. We also grabbed some of the free food.

We ate our food and then Mark went downstairs to use the bathroom.

While I waited for Mark to come back, I started talking to this mulatto girl. I'd never seen this girl at the Evergreen before. She said her name was Yvette.

Yvette and I talked for a few minutes. Then Mark came back.

"All right, let's get out of here," Mark said to me.

I turned to Yvette. "This is my buddy, Mark," I said.

"Hey," Mark said to Yvette.

"We're getting a room," I said. "Want to come with us and hang out?"

"Sure," Yvette said.

The three of us left the Evergreen and headed north on Yonge Street. All along Yonge, the sidewalks, which were already narrow, were crammed with people. People were coming from the Eaton Centre with huge bags, and boxes with stereos and VCRs in them. We passed a lot of stores where people were lined up outside, waiting to get in.

I wasn't interested in doing any Boxing Day shopping. Even though the deals were appealing—as we walked along Yonge Street, almost every store was offering at least fifty percent off—I didn't want to deal with crowds or have to wait in any lines. I knew the malls would be insane.

When we got to Carlton Street, we jumped onto a packed streetcar, and then headed west along College Street to Spadina Avenue. I had no idea where Spadina was. Mark was leading the way.

After about ten minutes on the streetcar, Mark turned to me, suddenly. "This is our stop," he said.

We all got off the streetcar. We crossed to the west side of Spadina Avenue and then walked over to the hotel. The Waverly was the second building from the corner, on the northwest side of the intersection. It was a white four-storey building.

Just by looking at the place, you could tell it was a dive. The white brick was dingy. In front of the place, hanging out underneath the awning above the door, were a couple of middle-aged hookers.

We passed the hookers and went into the hotel.

The hotel had a very small lobby. Mark and I went up to the front desk.

"Hey, how's it going?" I said to the clerk. "We want to get a double room here for the night."

The clerk told us the cost of the room. It was about fifty dollars, like Mark had told me, not including the refundable deposit for the room key.

"All right," I said.

Mark and I set down our squeegees. We reached into our pockets, counted up our change, and put what we needed down onto the counter. We both chipped in fifty-fifty. We paid mostly in loonies and toonies. I threw in a couple of five-dollar bills.

The clerk told us what room we'd be staying in. Then he gave us the key. "Check-out time is tomorrow morning at eleven o'clock," he said.

To exit the lobby, we had to walk up a couple of steps to a landing, and then open a door. On the other side of the door was a hallway. We walked down to the end of the hallway, to a really wide staircase, and then we walked up to our room on the third floor.

It was a fairly large hotel room. It had high ceilings and the same kind of speckled tile on the floor as in the stairwell and halls.

As soon as we got into the room, Mark turned on the TV. Then he sat down on one of the beds. Yvette and I sat down on the other bed. Before I even took off my coat, I took a dime of weed out of my pocket, rolled a joint and lit it up.

For the rest of the day, the three of us hung out in the room, watched TV, and smoked weed. The only time we left was to get food.

While we were hanging out in the room, every so often, this guy, who was staying in the room directly above ours, would start yelling all of a sudden. We knew that he was alone up there, yelling to himself, because we never heard any other voices up there, just this guy's.

"This is starting to get annoying," Yvette said after a while. "I hope he doesn't yell like this all night."

"Nah, he'll probably tire himself out pretty soon and go to bed," Mark said.

"I'm surprised the hotel hasn't kicked him out yet."

"In this dump? Anything fucking goes here, honey. Anyway, I don't think the guy can help it. I think he's got Tourette's or something."

When this guy yelled, you couldn't really make out, through the ceiling, what he was saying. It sounded like gibberish, though, with a lot of swearing.

"Anyway," Mark said, "I don't find it that annoying. We're just lucky that we didn't get a room near the Comfort Zone."

"What's that?" I said.

"It's an after-hours club. It's in the same building as the Waverly, but it's in the basement area. One time I got a room here and it was near the Comfort Zone. I had to listen to non-stop fucking gino beats all night. It was so bad, I couldn't even sleep."

That night, at around twelve thirty, we turned off the lights in the room. Yvette was in my bed, with me. We started to fool around under the covers, as we watched the end of some movie on TV.

Without having to persuade her at all, Yvette blew me. Then she let me fuck the hell out of her under the blanket. I hadn't gotten laid since I'd been in Toronto, so I really needed to get my rocks off. I didn't have a rubber, so I just made sure to pull out.

Once I got what I wanted from her, I kicked Yvette out of my bed. I sent her over to Mark's bed. "Ah, I'm tired," I said to her. "I want to go to bed now. You can go sleep with him, if you want."

Without even questioning it, Yvette got out of my bed, went over to Mark's bed and got under the blanket. Then she let Mark do her.

Man, what a little whore, I thought.

Yvette was a party girl, though. She knew how this shit worked. If she wanted to hang out in a hotel room for free, and smoke free weed all night with a couple of guys, then she was going to have to put out. Those were the rules.

After Mark and Yvette were done screwing, they went to sleep.

For a while, I watched TV. The movie was over now. The channel was airing an infomercial.

When I finally got tired, I shut my eyes and went to bed. I drifted off to the sound of the guy on the TV, droning on about a food processor, as the guy in the room above ours, with Tourette's, or whatever it was that he had, yelled on into the night . . .

The next morning, I got up at around six o'clock to take a piss. As I walked to the bathroom, I happened to glance over at Mark's bed and noticed that Yvette wasn't in it. I looked at the floor and saw that her purse and her shoes were gone from the room.

Hmm, I thought. The girl took off.

I really couldn't care less, though.

I went into the bathroom, took a piss, gave my dick a shake, and then went right back to bed.

When I got up again, it was eight thirty. Mark was still asleep.

I went to the bathroom and took a shower. When I got out of there a few minutes later, Mark was awake. He was sitting up in bed, watching TV, and smoking a cigarette.

"When did that chick take off?" Mark said to me.

"I don't know," I said. "I got up at around six to take a piss. She was already gone."

"I wouldn't have minded fucking her again."

"Me, too."

"Oh, well."

Mark and I stayed in the room until eleven o'clock, when it was time to check out. Since we'd paid for the room, we wanted to stay there every last minute.

Once we'd checked out, and we were outside the hotel, on Spadina Avenue, I turned to Mark. "Man, we should do this every night," I said. "It's so much better than staying at the fucking shelter."

In the hotel, Mark and I had freedom. We could do whatever the hell we wanted to do. We didn't have to abide by a curfew—the shelter had a 10:00 p.m. curfew—and follow a bunch of stupid rules.

"Yeah," Mark said. "That'll be the plan, then."

"How much money have you got left?" I said.

"Not enough to stay here another night," Mark said. "Not if I want to eat and smoke weed and all that."

"OK, well, let's go to the corner, then. We'll work until we've got enough money."

I started to walk towards College Street.

"We should take the Spadina streetcar to the subway," Mark said. "It'll be faster."

12

After that first day at the Waverly, Mark and I went there every day for about a week. Then, a few days into January, we ran into some trouble. Mark and I left the hotel at eleven o'clock in the morning. We got to Church and Bloor, started to work, and within half an hour, it started snowing. Suddenly, we couldn't make any money out there. Every car on the road had their windshield wipers going.

On the next three lights, we couldn't clean one window. We just stood there, at the corner, watching people's windshield wipers move back and forth.

Mark looked up at the sky. "I don't think this is going to stop anytime soon," he said.

The snow was coming down heavily. It was sticking to the road. The visibility was so low that you couldn't even see that far down Bloor Street.

Mark and I stood at the corner for a few more lights. Then we decided to leave. There was no point in staying. That was it for the workday.

"So much for going back to the hotel tonight," Mark said.

I still had some money left from the day before because I always made more money, squeegeeing, than Mark did. I could have gotten a room by myself there, but I didn't want to do this and then have to hang out alone all night. It would have been boring and kind of depressing, having no one to talk to all day. I decided that I would go back to Turning Point that night.

Mark and I dumped our water and then went our separate ways. I wanted to get out of the snow, so I headed over to College Park.

As I walked down Yonge Street, I looked at the traffic. It was crazy out on the road, as if everyone had forgotten how to drive in the snow. This was Toronto's first real snowfall of the winter. Prior to this, all we'd had were some flurries and a few dustings. People were driving like they'd forgotten how to drive in these weather conditions. They were driving too fast; they weren't giving themselves enough time to stop. Up the street, at the light, was a minor car accident. A car had rear-ended another car.

When I got to College Street, I went inside the mall and hung out in there for a while. At around two o'clock, I started to get hungry. I left the mall and headed over to the Evergreen. It was still snowing.

At the Evergreen, I got a bowl of soup, and then went to look for a table. It was crowded there that day. There weren't any free tables.

I looked around for someone that I recognized. There were a lot of French squeegee punks there that day. None of them could work, obviously, since it was snowing.

As I was scanning the room, I spotted the guy I'd met the first day I'd ever gone to the Evergreen—the guy who panhandled. I went over to the guy's table and asked if I could sit down.

The guy was eating spaghetti again. He looked up at me. "Yeah, sure," he said. "How've you been? I haven't seen you in a while."

This guy obviously didn't come to the Evergreen too often. Or maybe he did, but we were just never there at the same time. I didn't always see the same people when I went there. Because it was a drop-in centre, I'd see certain people only once in a while.

The panhandler guy and I made some small talk while we ate. I didn't really feel like socializing too much, though. I was kind of in a bad mood. I was annoyed that it was snowing and that I'd had to quit working so early. I'd really just gone there for the five-cent soup.

I mentioned this to the panhandler—how I'd had to quit working that morning because of the weather. He told me that, with panhandling, you actually made more money when it snowed. "People feel sorrier for you when they see you sitting there, in the snow," he told me.

Well, that makes sense, I thought.

The guy started to tell me about his day. "I made fifty bucks in a couple of hours this morning," he said. "I was having a pretty good day. Then this psycho guy who I've never seen before comes by and gives me this bag from Tim Hortons. You know what was in it?"

"No, what?" I said.

"Donuts. But the donuts had bite marks in them. Can you fucking believe that? This guy went out of his way to buy a couple of donuts, and then he fucking took a single bite out of each one and gave them to a guy panning."

"Some people are assholes."

"Most people are actually all right."

The guy started to tell me about all the regulars who helped him out on a daily basis. "Then I'll get these random people who give me stuff," he said. "That's how I got these Jordans."

The guy brought his foot out from underneath the table to show me the shoes that he was wearing.

I looked down at the shoes. They were Air Jordans.

"Yeah, those are nice," I said.

"And they've barely been worn," the guy said. "A black guy gave them to me. The only thing about them is they're about a size too small for me. They're an eight. I take a size nine."

"Give them away, then."

"Yeah, I think I'm going to have to do that. I'm starting to get foot pain. I think I'm going to go downstairs to the foot clinic."

In the basement of the Evergreen was a free foot clinic. It was next to the free health clinic and the bathrooms.

"Have you ever gone there?" the guy said.

"To the foot clinic?" I said. "No."

"You should. It's pretty good. They give you free shoes and shit."

We were both done eating by this point, so we got up, brought our bowls to the counter, and then went outside to have a smoke.

As soon as we got outside, the panhandler told me that he couldn't find his smokes. "Shit," he said, as he checked all of his pockets. "I just bought that pack this morning."

The guy immediately turned to me. "Hey, could I bum a smoke off you?" he said.

I knew the guy was full of shit. He'd never bought a pack of smokes that morning; he just wanted to bum one off me.

"Sorry, but I've only got one left," I said.

This was true. I really did only have one cigarette left.

"That's OK," the guy said. He turned and immediately asked someone else out there for a smoke. The person he asked gave him one.

For a few minutes, we stood out there, smoking and watching people walk down Yonge Street. It had stopped snowing. The sidewalk had already been cleared. All over it were chunks of salt.

I didn't really feel like hanging out at the Evergreen anymore, so when I finished my smoke, I told the guy that I was going to get going.

"All right, I'll see you around," the guy said.

For a while, I just walked around downtown. The sky was clearing up, but the air still felt heavy and damp.

As I walked, I noticed that the sidewalks along the major roads had been cleared and salted already. The city had cleared them fast.

I stopped at a light somewhere. As I stood there, waiting for the light to change, I suddenly found myself wondering how long the light was.

Is this light longer than the one at Church and Bloor? I wondered. Could this be a good place to squeegee?

Now that I'd been squeegeeing for a couple of weeks, I was starting to notice how long traffic lights were when I was at them. Without even realizing it, I was paying attention to this stuff. It was just like on the carnival, when I'd first started working there. I'd walk down the midway on my breaks and I'd pay attention to what everyone else was doing, who worked in a game. That was how I learned a lot of what I knew.

No sooner had I asked myself this question, the light changed. I decided that the light at Church and Bloor was longer.

That night, I went back to the shelter early, when they let everyone in for the night. Because I hadn't been there in about a week, I wanted to make sure that I'd have a bed.

I talked to the staff at the door, over the intercom.

"Hey, it's me, Jim," I said. "Do you guys have a bed for me? I don't have anywhere else to stay tonight."

"Yes, we've got beds available," Andrew said. "Hold on, Jim. I'll buzz you in."

In the morning, the weather was good. I ran into Mark at the shelter and we went out and squeegeed.

Not long after we got out there, some asshole motorist rolled down his window on a light, while I was walking down the lineup, looking for a car.

"Hey, you're supposed to be homeless?" the guy said to me. "You're wearing Adidas shoes. *I* can't even afford Adidas shoes."

I couldn't believe the nerve of this guy, rolling down his window just to say this to me.

I immediately walked over to the guy's car. As soon as the guy saw me coming, he started to roll up his window, like he was worried that I was going to attack him through the gap. It was one of those hand crank ones, so he couldn't roll it up that fast.

I got to the car before the guy managed to get his window up.

"Yeah, I'm wearing Adidas," I said. "But, unlike you, buddy, *I* don't have a twenty thousand-dollar car. I'm on my feet all day. I need to wear good shoes. What would you rather me do, go spend all my money on booze and drugs?"

The guy got his window rolled up as I was talking. He wouldn't even make eye contact with me now. He looked like he wanted nothing more than for the light to turn green, and for me to go away.

"Fucking asshole," I muttered.

I went back to the curb, as the light changed. I watched the guy drive away.

"What was that all about?" Mark said.

"Ah, some guy just made some fucking crack to me about my shoes," I said.

Later that morning, while Mark and I were working, some guy came by with a squeegee sticking out of his backpack. He was young. He looked like a teenage runaway or something.

Mark and I thought the guy wanted to jump in and squeegee. "Sorry, no one else at this corner," Mark immediately told the guy. "This is our corner. We're here every morning."

This was the first time since I'd been out there with Mark that we'd had to deal with some other squeegee kid at our corner. Mark and I were always there so early in the morning that when we got there, there was never anyone else there.

"I just want to hang out," the guy said.

"Oh," I said.

"OK," Mark said. "All right."

Because the guy wasn't a punker, and because he wasn't French, we let him hang out with us. In between lights, we all stood at the corner and talked. The guy's name, we found out, was Scottie. He told us that he was seventeen years old. He looked a lot younger to me, though. He looked about fifteen.

While we worked, Scottie told us that he usually worked down by the Gardiner Expressway. He didn't work every day, just here and there.

"Wow, this is a really long light," Scottie said.

"Yeah, it's ninety seconds long," I said.

"I think it's the longest light I've seen in this city."

Scottie hung out with us for a while. Then he took off.

At around ten thirty, Mark left, too.

"I'll be back at noon," Mark told me. "Then we'll go to the hotel, OK?"

At noon, Mark wasn't back yet, so I just took off. I wasn't going to stand around, waiting for the guy. I went to Foot Locker in the Eaton Centre, instead, and blew a hundred bucks in there on some more Adidas clothes.

The next morning, I ran into Mark at the shelter.

"What happened to you yesterday?" I said.

"What do you mean?" Mark said.

"You said you were going to come back at noon. You never came back."

"Oh, yeah. Sorry. That was because of this fucking guy. I gave him money and he went to get me some dope. It took him forever to fucking come back."

Mark and I walked over to our corner. We got something to eat, got our bucket, and then got to work.

I was hoping to go back to the Waverly that night, but Mark and I didn't end up going there. That morning, while we were working, Mark took off again and didn't come back.

Over the next week, Mark and I only ended up going to the Waverly a couple of times. Because I was consistently at the corner all morning on the days that we weren't at the hotel—I wasn't taking off early like Mark to get drugs—I started to get some regulars. It was always the same cars at the light, I noticed. It was always the same people on their way to work. Some people let me wash their windows for free the whole week, and at the end of the week, they gave me a five-, ten-, or twenty-dollar bill.

Even though Mark was taking off early a lot, Scottie was coming by here and there to hang out, so I wasn't always alone at the corner.

One morning, while Mark was gone, Scottie asked me if he could jump in and work until Mark got back.

"Yeah, go ahead," I said.

For about an hour, Scottie and I worked alongside each other at the corner.

At noon, Mark wasn't back yet. I told Scottie that I was taking off.

"All right," Scottie said. "I'm going to stay here and keep working."

"That's fine," I said. "If Mark doesn't come back, though, before you leave, could you return the bucket for us?"

"Yeah, sure. Where do I bring it?"

"Just go inside the building there and bring it to the coffee shop. Give it to whoever's behind the counter."

"All right."

"OK, thanks."

13

A couple of weeks into January, we got another snow storm. I was on the balcony at the shelter one morning, having a smoke, when all of a sudden it started to snow.

I looked at the snow falling down from the sky beyond the awning of the balcony. Ah, shit, I thought to myself. Guess I ain't working today.

I ran into Russ as I was leaving the shelter that morning. "Hey, want to go get a coffee?" I said. "I can't work today. It's snowing."

"OK," Russ said.

Russ and I walked over to the Second Cup by the Evergreen. We each got a coffee, and then we went across the street to College Park and walked through the mall to stay out of the snow.

We hung around in the mall for a while, and then Russ told me that he wanted to go check his mail.

"I'll come with you," I said. "I need to check mine, too."

I hadn't checked my P.O. Box since I'd gotten it, in December. It hadn't been six weeks yet since I did my taxes, but it was getting close. I was hoping my tax refund had come early.

When we got to the post office, Russ and I checked our mail. My box was empty.

I looked over at Russ. He had some mail.

"No mail?" Russ said, as he closed his box and locked it.

"No," I said. "I'm still waiting on my tax refund. I was hoping it had come early."

"Yeah, it takes a while."

Russ and I left the post office. We smoked a joint in a nearby park, and then Russ told me that he had to go do some stuff. As usual, he didn't elaborate in terms of what he had to do.

"OK, I'll see you tonight, back at the shelter," I said.

"Yeah, have a good one," Russ said.

I walked down the street, feeling kind of disappointed. I was really hoping that my tax refund had been there. I was getting impatient for it. I decided that I should start checking my box every few days now. It was getting close to the six-week mark.

The day after it snowed, it got really cold suddenly. The temperature dropped from around zero degrees one day to around minus fifteen the next day.

That morning, I left the shelter with Mark to go squeegee. As we walked over to the corner, I thought about how cold it was outside and how we would be putting water on people's windows.

"I think we should get some windshield washer fluid with de-icer in it," I said. "If we don't, I'm thinking the water is going to freeze on people's windows."

"All right," Mark said.

When we got to our corner, we hung out in the building that the coffee shop was in for about fifteen minutes, and then we walked over to the Canadian Tire.

We got to the store just as it was opening. We went inside and went straight to the aisle where the windshield washer fluids were.

Mark had obviously never driven before in his life because he had no idea which one to get.

I grabbed a jug off the shelf. "It's this one," I said.

The stuff was blue and came in a four-gallon jug. It was good for down to minus thirty-five degrees Celsius, the label said.

The washer fluid was only a few bucks. I'd picked a cheaper brand. We each chipped in for it, and then we left the store and walked back to Bloor Street.

When we got back to Bloor, we went into the coffee shop. We got something to eat and then we went to the front to ask for a bucket.

"Can you just fill it up halfway today?" I said to the guy.

"Just halfway?" the guy said.

"Yeah."

"OK. No problem."

The guy went into the kitchen. He came back a minute later with a five-gallon bucket half-full of water.

"Thanks," I said.

"See you boys later," the guy said.

I took the bucket. Mark had the jug of washer fluid.

As soon as we got outside, I put the bucket down on the ground. Then I turned to Mark. "OK, just fill it up the rest of the way with that shit," I said.

Mark opened the jug and then poured the blue stuff into the bucket.

We still had some washer fluid left over. We were going to end up chucking the rest of it because we didn't need it, but we held onto it for the time being. We brought it with us to the curb.

Mark and I worked straight through until noon. We didn't stop once to go inside and warm up. We were getting a lot of tips from drivers who felt sorry for us that we were out there, working in such cold weather. I was getting some five- and ten-dollar bills.

At one point, it looked like Mark was starting to get cold.

"Go inside and warm up," I said.

"Are you going to go inside, too?" Mark said.

"No, I want to keep working. The money's good. This ain't that cold to me, really. I'm from Alberta."

At noon, when Mark and I finished work, we chucked what we had left of the washer fluid. Then we went over to the Evergreen to eat for five cents. We hung out there for a while, bought some weed, and then we took the TTC to Spadina and College and got a double room at the Waverly. We hadn't gone there for a few days. It was nice going back to the hotel.

In the morning, when Mark and I got up, there was snow on the ground. It wasn't snowing anymore, though. The sky was cloudless and blue.

Even though the weather was fine, I decided that I wasn't going to go out and squeegee. I felt like having a day off. I'd been working almost every day since I'd started squeegeeing. I felt like I deserved a day off.

We stayed in the hotel room until eleven o'clock. Mark wanted to go to the corner to work.

"OK," I said. "Have fun."

"Oh, loads," Mark said.

We left the hotel and jumped on the College streetcar together. When we got to Yonge Street, we went our separate ways. Mark went into the subway to catch a northbound train to Bloor-Yonge Station. I headed down Yonge Street on foot.

Because I still had money on me, I decided to go to Foot Locker in the Eaton Centre. I had a lot of clothes already because I'd been going there almost every day since I'd started squeegeeing, blowing a hundred bucks each time, but I just wanted more shit. I didn't want to have to wear the same thing all the time. The store was constantly getting new stock. Now that it was the middle of January, they were starting to get not so much winter stuff anymore, but stuff for the next season.

That day at Foot Locker, I saw this really nice Adidas jacket. I was still buying all-Adidas. It was a bomber style, reversible jacket with the trademark three stripes around the collar. It had stitching on it that looked like little diamonds all over the coat. It wasn't a different colour stitch or anything, it was just black thread. But the way that the squares were set, on their sides, they looked like diamonds.

I looked at the price tag. "Whoa," I said.

The coat was two hundred dollars.

I immediately put the coat back on the rack. I didn't have two hundred dollars on me, so it wasn't like I could have bought it, but even if I'd had the money, I still wouldn't have bought it. That was just way too much money, I felt, to spend on coat, especially one that wasn't leather and that wasn't made for winter. It was more of a fall-type coat. It was too cold outside to wear it yet anyway.

I bought something else—an Adidas shirt and a backpack. As soon as I got outside the store, I tore off the price tag on the backpack, shoved the shirt into it, and then slung the bag over my shoulder.

That night, I went back to the shelter early to make sure that I'd have a bed.

Vadim, one of the staff, buzzed me in, but when I walked in the door, he immediately called me over to the window.

"Yeah, what is it, Vadim?" I said.

"I didn't want to turn you away," Vadim said. "But we don't actually have a bed for you, Jim. This is totally against the rules, and I shouldn't even be letting you do this, but I'm going to let you sleep on a couch here, tonight."

I was surprised that the shelter was full.

"It happens sometimes," Vadim told me. "Especially in the winter months, when it's really cold outside. It's been cold these last few days. We've been seeing an above average number of people here, at the shelter."

I didn't care that I had to sleep on a couch. I was just happy to hear that I wasn't being turned away. I didn't want to have to go find another shelter. I had no money on me, so this is what I would have had to do.

"Thanks," I said. "You have no idea how much you're helping me out right now."

"Just don't tell anyone that I let you sleep on the couch, OK?" Vadim said. "Let's keep this between us. In the morning, just make sure that you're up before everyone else, so that no one sees you out there."

"What about the night staff? They're going to see me sleeping on the couch."

"It's not the staff I'm worried about. I'll explain the situation to them. They'll understand. It'll be fine. You're a regular here. We all know you. You don't cause any trouble. I just don't want anyone *else* to know, if you know what I mean."

"Oh, you mean, like, the other guys staying here?"

"Yes. If it gets out that we let you sleep on the couch, then the next time we're full, people are going to want us to let them do the same thing. We don't want to establish a precedent."

"OK. Got it. Don't worry, Vadim. I won't say anything to anyone. I really appreciate it, though, man. You're a good guy."

That night, when it was time for lights out, I slipped out onto the balcony while everyone else went upstairs to go to bed. I hung out there for about ten minutes, had a smoke, and then went back inside.

It was dark in the living room. It felt weird being in there alone, with the lights and the TV turned off.

I laid down on one of the couches. I didn't have a pillow or a blanket or anything, so I curled up on my side and put my hands under my head. It wasn't the most comfortable way to sleep. The couch felt kind of scratchy. It also smelled like it needed to be cleaned.

Even though I'd taken a day off from squeegeeing, I was tired once I laid down and closed my eyes. Within a few minutes, I was asleep.

14

The cold weather didn't last long. Within a few days, it got warmer. We had a brief thaw, and then the temperature went back down to a couple of degrees below zero.

One morning, I was out squeegeeing with Mark, when I started to feel itchy, suddenly. As I worked, I couldn't stop scratching my forearms and the backs of my hands.

"You need to stop doing that," Mark said to me.

"Doing what?" I said.

"Scratching. You're starting to make *me* feel itchy."

I would have stopped scratching if I could have, but I couldn't help it. I was insanely itchy. The more I scratched, the more I wanted to scratch.

"If it bothers you so much, then look the other way," I told Mark. "I'm fucking itchy, man. I can't help it."

For the rest of the day, I struggled with this itchy feeling.

I knew right away that something was up. There was no way that I could be this itchy without there being a good reason for it. I started to wonder if maybe I'd caught something from sleeping on that couch, that night at the shelter. I started to think lice, but my scalp wasn't itchy. It was just the backs of my hands and my forearms. I couldn't figure it out.

That night, when I got back to the shelter, I talked to the staff about it.

"I don't know what's causing it," I said to Andrew. "I'm so itchy. I feel like I'm going crazy."

"Well, I don't know for sure, but to me it sounds like scabies," Andrew said.

Andrew said this like it was just a run-of-the-mill thing. "We see cases of scabies quite a lot in the shelter system," he told me. "It's fairly common. As staff, we try to be careful when we're doing laundry and things like that."

"What is it?" I said.

"It's a skin infestation by a mite. These mites make track-like burrows, or tunnels, in the skin and that's where they lay their eggs. You'd have to go to a doctor to find out for sure if you have them, but based on your symptoms, Jim, I'm pretty sure that's what you have."

Eggs? I thought. Tunnels?

I could almost feel my skin crawl.

"How do you think I got this?" I said.

"It's hard to say," Andrew said. "You can get it through direct skin-to-skin contact with an infected person, or through contact with something that's contaminated, like clothing, for instance, or bedding."

Bedding, I thought. I must have gotten it from that couch.

"So, how do I get rid of these mites?" I said.

"There's an over-the-counter treatment that you can buy," Andrew said. "You can get it at any drug store. It's a cream. It comes in a tube. You put it all over yourself at night, wash it off in the morning, and that's it. It's a one-time treatment. It kills everything in one shot."

"OK. I'm going to go get the stuff."

"All right. We'll change all of your bedding tonight before lights out."

I immediately left the shelter and went to a nearby drugstore on Wellesley Street. I went straight to the back, to the pharmacy, and asked the pharmacist if the store carried the treatment for scabies.

"Yes, we carry that," the pharmacist said. He was an old guy. He seemed a little hard of hearing.

The pharmacist told me the name of the product. Then he told me where to find it. "It's in aisle seven," he said. "It's right next to the head lice shampoo."

The guy couldn't have said this any louder. A couple of people turned and looked at me.

"Yes, thank you," I said. Then I turned and walked away.

I found the treatment in aisle seven. I paid for it and then went back to the shelter.

Before I even looked at the box that the treatment came in, the first thing I did was wash all of my clothes. Andrew hadn't told me to do this, but it was common sense. If the staff were going to change my bedding, it didn't make sense to get into bed wearing infested clothes.

Luckily, it was early enough in the evening that I had time to do all my laundry. I had Vadim open my locker—I had a full-sized locker at the shelter, which only the staff had the key to—and then I took everything out of it and washed it all in hot water. I had a lot of clothes. I had enough for two full loads. My winter coat, by itself, though, took up a big portion of a load.

Once I'd washed and dried everything, I went to the bathroom to apply the treatment. I went into one of the shower stalls, stripped down to my bare ass, and then read the instructions on the label.

"Apply a thin layer of cream over the entire body, from the neck down to the toes, once at bedtime," the label said. "Leave on for between eight to fourteen hours, and then remove with soap and water."

I squeezed a big glob of cream into the palm of my hand, rubbed my hands together, and then spread the cream over my entire body.

Once the cream had dried a bit, I put on a fresh pair of clothes. The clothes I'd been wearing went into a plastic Foot Locker bag that I'd had in my locker. I tied the bag and then double knotted it.

That night, when I went to sleep, I kept thinking about little bugs burrowing under my skin. I wondered if the treatment was going to work because I still felt really itchy.

Whatever you do, don't scratch yourself, I said to myself. You don't want to scratch off this goddamn cream.

15

Within a couple of days, I wasn't itchy anymore. I wasn't completely sure that I'd even had scabies because I'd never gone to a doctor, but the over-the-counter treatment had worked, so I figured that's what I'd had.

This wasn't the end of my health problems, however. About a week after I got scabies, I woke up in the morning, feeling like I was coming down with a cold.

I left the shelter with Mark that morning and walked over to Church and Bloor. I didn't care if I wasn't feeling well. I needed money. I had to go out and work.

As we walked down Wellesley Street to Church Street, I started coughing. It was one of those gross, phlegmy-sounding coughs.

"Ugh, that sounds healthy," Mark said.

I spit out what I'd coughed up onto the ground. It was a glob of greenish-coloured mucus.

"I feel like shit today," I said. "I think I'm coming down with something, man."

It was the middle of winter now—the last week of January. A lot of people were walking around with colds, I'd noticed. A few days earlier, at the Evergreen, some guy had been blowing his nose and coughing his head off. I told Mark about this. "I think I caught that guy's cold," I said.

"Yeah, there's some real nasty shit going around right now," Mark said.

When we got to our corner, we went to the coffee shop and got something to eat. I had a breakfast sandwich. Mark had the same. We sat down at one of the tables to eat our food.

Once I started eating, I didn't have much of an appetite. I didn't know if it was from the grease from the bacon on the sandwich or what, but as I was eating, I started to feel sick to my stomach. I couldn't eat any more.

"Not hungry?" Mark said.

"I don't know," I said. "My stomach's bothering me all of a sudden."

"Yeah, you've definitely got some kind of bug. Whatever you do, try not to cough on me, OK? I don't want to get your germs."

"Oh, slow down."

"I'm kidding."

"No you're not."

I waited for Mark to finish eating. When he was done, we went up to the counter, got our bucket, and then we went outside to go work.

As I worked, I kept coughing up mucus. Every time I coughed, some of it came up. I felt sluggish out there. I felt like I was moving in slow motion. I wanted to work, I just didn't have it in me, physically. I could only get one car done on a light.

I only lasted about an hour. At around nine o'clock, I decided that I'd had enough. I was feeling feverish. I was still feeling sick to my stomach. I was coughing up even more green mucus.

"I'm out of here," I said to Mark.

"You're taking off for the day?" Mark said.

"Yeah, I just can't do this today. It's like torture."

The light changed. Mark took his squeegee out of the bucket. "OK," he said. "Take it easy." Then he walked into the road.

I left the corner and walked over to the Eaton Centre. For a while, I just walked around the mall.

By the afternoon, I was feeling pretty rough. I felt like I had the worst flu I'd ever had in my life. My muscles were sore. I had chills. I felt like I was burning up. Because it was Saturday, I couldn't even go to the Evergreen because the place wasn't open on the weekends. I had to hang out in the mall. I had nowhere else to go because I didn't want to be outside. It was miserable being stuck in that mall all day, though, walking around, sitting on benches. All I wanted was to lie down in a bed and go to sleep.

That night, I went back to the shelter early, as soon as the staff started to let people in. I didn't eat any dinner. I'd vomited on the way over to the shelter and I didn't think I could keep anything down.

While everyone sat in the kitchen area, eating, I sat in the living room, on one of the couches. Most of the couches faced the TV, but there was this one couch that backed onto another couch, and which faced the other way, where the payphone was. The payphone was right by the office window, at the front, where you came in.

I sat on the couch, feeling so sick, I felt like I was in outer space. My head was killing me from coughing all day. It was like a pressure sensation.

Suddenly, some guy came up to me. I'd seen this guy around at the shelter, but I'd never talked to him. He was all pissed off about something.

"What are you looking at?" the guy said to me.

"Huh?" I said.

I had no idea what this guy was talking about. I hadn't even realized he'd been standing there until he'd started talking. My eyes hadn't been focused on anything. I'd just been sitting there, on the couch, staring off into space.

"The whole time I was on the phone, you were sitting here, staring at me," the guy said. "What are you, a fucking faggot or something?"

I immediately snapped out of the stupor I was in. "I wasn't looking at *you*," I said. "I wasn't looking at *anything*. I was just sitting here, staring into space. I'm not feeling good, OK? I'm sick. Call me a fag again, though, motherfucker. Even though I'm sick, I'll get up right now and kick you right in your fucking head."

I was bluffing, of course. I barely had the energy to get up off the couch, let alone kick this guy's ass. Like most bullies, though, as soon as I got up in the guy's face, he immediately backed down and put his tail between his legs.

"Yeah, whatever," the guy said. Then he turned and walked away.

I kept sitting there, on the couch. No one else bothered me or used the phone.

As I sat there, I started to worry. I'd never been this sick before. I didn't even get sick that often. I was the type of person who'd get sick maybe once a year. Either this was the worst flu I'd ever had or it was something else, I thought to myself. Something in my gut told me that it wasn't the flu, though, that it was something more serious. I had this feeling that I should go to the hospital.

I didn't know where the nearest hospital was, so I got up and went to the office window. Vadim was sitting in there, doing some paperwork.

"Hey, Vadim, I'm feeling really sick," I said. "Could you tell me where the nearest hospital is?"

Vadim looked up at me from his desk. "Whoa, you really don't look good," he said. "You're as white as a ghost. Jim, I think I should call you an ambulance."

I didn't want an ambulance. I didn't need the paramedics coming in there and making a spectacle out of all this.

"No, please don't do that," I said. "I don't need an ambulance. I can get there on my own. You just need to tell me where to go."

I could see that Vadim still wanted to call the ambulance for me, but he wasn't going to argue with me, I could see that. He probably knew that I wouldn't have stayed there anyway, had he done this. I would have just walked right out the door.

"Well, Women's College Hospital would be the closest one to here," Vadim said.

"OK," I said. "Where's that?"

"It's on Grenville Street, near Bay Street. It's about a fifteen-minute walk."

I had no idea where Grenville was. I still didn't know the streets in Toronto that well. They weren't like the streets in

Edmonton, where each one was either a street or an avenue, and each one had a number. In Toronto, the streets all had names. Lots of times when I was out, walking around, I'd take a wrong turn and get lost.

"Grenville is one street north of College," Vadim said.

I must have looked confused because Vadim gave me some further directions.

As Vadim was talking to me, Russ just happened to walk in the door to the shelter.

"Russ," Vadim said. He motioned for Russ to come up to the window.

"Yeah, Vadim," Russ said. "What's up?"

Russ turned to me. "Oh, hey, Jim," he said. He immediately noticed how sick I looked. "Are you all right?" he said. "You don't look too good."

"No, I'm sick," I said.

"Russ, could you do me a favour?" Vadim said.

"Yeah, what?" Russ said.

"Could you please take Jim to the hospital? He doesn't know where to go. You know where Women's College is, right?"

"Yeah," Russ said. "Why, what's wrong with him?"

"We don't know," Vadim said. "But he's really ill. He needs to go to Emergency right away."

"All right, I'll take him. I know where to go."

I left the shelter with Russ. We walked along Wellesley Street to Bay Street, and then walked south on Bay to Grenville. The hospital was a block west of Bay. It was a tall building with brown brick.

Russ took me into the ER. I went up to the front and checked in with the hospital staff. I showed the person admitting me my Alberta Health, which was just a piece of paper that I had in my wallet. This was my provincial health insurance.

The next thing I did was talk to a nurse.

"What symptoms have you been having?" the nurse asked me.

I told the nurse all my symptoms.

"Are you having any trouble breathing?" the nurse said.

"No, I can breathe fine," I said.

"Do you have any chest pain?"

"No. I just have a pain in my head from coughing so much."

"OK, and how long have you had these symptoms for?"

"Since this morning. It started out with a cough and a sick feeling in my stomach, and it just got worse and worse as the day went on—literally, by the hour."

The nurse took notes as I talked. When she finished her questions, she told me to have a seat in the waiting area and to wait for my name to be called.

Russ sat with me.

"You don't have to stay," I said.

"It's all right," Russ said. "I don't mind. If they don't keep you here overnight, I can help you get back to the shelter."

The ER was packed. There were tons of people sitting in there, waiting for their names to be called. I didn't end up waiting too long. Because of my symptoms, they called my name pretty quickly.

Right away, I had a chest x-ray done. Russ came with me to the imaging department. He waited for me in the waiting area.

After I had the x-ray, I was taken to another room. Russ came with me into the room. I sat down on the examination table. Russ sat in a plastic chair.

"The doctor will be with you shortly," the nurse told us. Then she left the room.

In about ten minutes, the doctor appeared at the door. He took my chart from outside the door and looked at it, as he walked into the room.

"You've got pneumonia," the doctor told me. "The x-ray showed some fluid in your left lung. We're going to keep you here, in the hospital, OK? We'll be putting you on some strong antibiotics to kill this infection."

The doctor examined me quickly. He felt my neck, and then he looked at my ears and throat. Then he had me lift up my shirt, so that he could listen to me breathe with his stethoscope.

"I hear some wheezing," the doctor said.

"I've got asthma," I said. "I wheeze a bit sometimes."

"Are you having any trouble breathing right now? Any shortness of breath?"

"No. I just feel really sick. I keep coughing up all this nasty mucus."

"Green or yellow mucus?"

"Yeah."

"That's from the infection in your lung."

The doctor made some notes in my chart. "The nurse will be with you in a moment," he said. Then he left the room.

In a few minutes, the nurse arrived. She brought me to a semi-private room on an upper floor.

Russ stayed with me right up until I got to my room. At this point, the nurse turned to him and told him that it was time for him to leave.

"Don't worry, your friend is in good hands," the nurse

said. "He needs to rest, though. You can come back tomorrow and see him during visiting hours."

"OK, I'll see you," Russ said to me.

"All right," I said. "Bye."

As soon as Russ left, the nurse hooked me up to an IV drip. That was how the antibiotics were going to be given to me—intravenously.

"If you need anything, just ring the bell," the nurse said. "We'll hear it in the nurses' station. Someone will come to your room."

"OK," I said.

The nurse turned off the light, and then left the room. As soon as she was gone, I closed my eyes and tried to sleep.

As I was lying there, feeling sick as hell and trying to drift off, I thought about how well things had been going for me with the squeegeeing. Now, I was out of commission, in the hospital.

I should have saved my money, I thought.

That was the worst part of all of this. I'd been making big money, squeegeeing, but I'd been spending it as fast as I was making it.

The next day I still felt really sick. I could barely eat anything. I didn't have much of an appetite. Anything I did manage to eat, I couldn't keep down.

It didn't help that everything I ate tasted exactly the same. No matter what I ate or tried to eat, it all tasted the same, like garbage.

I asked the nurse about this when she was in my room, doing her rounds.

"How come everything I eat tastes the same?" I said.

"It's because of the antibiotics you're on," the nurse said. "They affect your sense of taste."

"Well, it's making me not want to eat anything."

"I know, hon."

The nurse looked at the food I had left on my tray. "Try to eat a little more," she said.

I had a couple more bites. As soon as the nurse left the room, I pushed the tray aside.

On my third day in the hospital, Russ came to visit me. I was surprised to see him.

"How are you feeling?" Russ said.

"Like shit," I said.

Russ sat in the chair near my bed. He noticed the tray of food I hadn't finished. "Didn't eat your lunch?" he said.

"That's as much as I could eat," I said. "The IV drip they've got me on has some kind of antibiotics in it that make everything taste the same. It doesn't matter what I eat, it all tastes like garbage. Half the time, I'm throwing it back up."

Russ looked at the IV in my hand. "Want me to yank that thing out for you?" he said.

I shook my head and laughed. "Smart ass," I said.

"You know me," Russ said.

"Yeah, well, I need a laugh. It fucking sucks, being stuck in this hospital bed, man."

"I think I know what might cheer you up."

"Oh, yeah? What?"

"You know that cheque you've been waiting on?"

"My tax refund?"

"Yeah. I think you finally got it. I was at the post office this morning. I just happened to notice that there was something in your P.O. Box. You know how you can see inside the box a little bit from the outside?"

"Yeah."

"Well, there was a brown envelope in there. Government shit's always in a brown envelope."

I knew it had to be my tax refund. I had nothing else going to that P.O. Box.

It was obvious that Russ was a pretty decent person. He'd gone out of his way to come to the hospital and tell me this.

"Thanks," I said.

"Yeah, no problem," Russ said. "I knew you'd been waiting on that money. I just thought I'd come here and let you know."

Russ stayed for a few more minutes. Then he told me that he had to go. "Well, anyway, I just came here to see how you were doing, and to tell you about your mail," he said.

"All right," I said. "See you later."

"Try to eat something, OK?"

"I will."

After Russ left, I watched some TV. As I sat in my bed, flipping through the channels, I started to think about my tax refund. Now that I knew it had arrived, I wanted to go get it. Just knowing that I had that cheque in my P.O. Box, made me literally start to feel better. I suddenly felt like I was well enough to leave the hospital.

The nurse came into my room at around three o'clock in the afternoon. She was doing her rounds.

"I'm feeling a lot better now," I said to the nurse. "I think I'm ready to leave."

The nurse had this look of shock on her face. "Oh, no," she said. "You're not ready to leave yet, hon. We can't discharge you until you can keep down solid food."

As soon as the nurse said this, I picked up the tray of

food that I hadn't finished eating and started to eat. The food was cold now. It was even less appetizing than it had been when it had first been served to me. It was tomato soup and a grilled cheese sandwich. My sense of taste was so screwed up that if I'd been blindfolded, I wouldn't have been able to tell what food I was eating.

I forced myself to eat every last scrap of food on the tray. Somehow, I managed to hold it down.

Within two days of Russ coming to see me, I was keeping down solid food.

I told the hospital that I wanted to leave and they released me. They wanted me to stay longer, but because I was keeping down solid food, they couldn't keep me there any longer if I didn't want to be there.

As soon as I was discharged, I went straight to the Canada Post outlet to get my cheque.

When I got there, I opened my P.O. Box, took out the brown envelope, and immediately tore it open.

The cheque was for almost three grand.

Woo-hoo, I thought.

16

Once I'd cashed my cheque and the excitement of getting all that money had worn off, I realized that I hadn't fully recovered yet from the pneumonia. The next day, when I woke up in the morning, I felt kind of blah. The illness had drained me, I realized. I was still in recovery mode. Luckily, I had a bunch of money now and I didn't have to work. I could take it easy.

One night in early February, not long after I'd gotten out of the hospital, I was sitting in the living room at the shelter, while the staff handed out the personal needs allowances. Even though I'd been squeegeeing up until I'd gotten sick, I'd never stopped collecting the PNA.

The staff must have realized that I was working when they saw me leaving the shelter in the mornings with a squeegee, but they never asked me about. They didn't care, obviously, if you had some kind of hustles going on in the street. If you told them that you were unemployed, they just gave you the PNA.

The staff called my name. I went up to the window, got my envelope with my twenty-one dollars in it, and then sat back down in the living room.

When the staff were done calling out the names, I turned to the guy who was sitting next to me. He was an acquaintance of mine. "Hey, how come they never called you up to the window?" I said.

"Because I don't get the PNA," the guy said.

"Why not? Oh, you told them you're working, I guess."

"No. It's because I get a street allowance from welfare."

I'd never heard of this.

"What's that?" I said.

"It's an emergency welfare cheque. It's what they give to people who are on the street, who don't have an address."

"Is it more than the PNA?"

"Yeah. It's a lot more. It works out to about an extra hundred bucks a month. You can go right to the welfare office every month and get an emergency cheque for a hundred and ninety bucks, or you can take about ninety dollars a month from here."

And here I was, like an idiot, collecting twenty-one dollars a week, I thought.

"If you have all of your ID, it makes more sense to get welfare," the guy said. "You just can't collect both at the same time. The shelter doesn't want you to collect the PNA if you're getting a welfare cheque."

I had all of my government-issued ID on me, in my wallet. I could have gone to the welfare office and applied for a street allowance at any time.

"So, where's the welfare office?" I said.

I couldn't believe what the guy told me. "It's next door to Turning Point," he said.

"You're kidding me?" I said. "Next door?"

"Yeah. It's in that building right on the corner of Jarvis and Wellesley. You know the one that says '111' on it?"

"Yeah."

"That's the building. You just go in there and go up to the second floor. As soon as you step out of the elevator, you're literally right in the welfare office."

It was too fucking much. I just couldn't believe it. I'd been at Turning Point all this time, and all I had to do to get a hundred and ninety dollars a month was go right next door.

The next morning, I left the shelter at eight o'clock and went straight to the welfare office. I was going to go see about getting this emergency cheque.

I walked into the building at the corner of Jarvis and Wellesley. Right at the front, when you walked in the door, was a desk with a security guard sitting behind it. I walked past the desk to the end of the hall, and then took the elevator up to the second floor.

I'd never been to a welfare office before in my life, so I had no idea what to expect. I was a little taken aback when I walked in there and saw that the clerks were all sitting behind this huge pane of glass. I'd never seen anything like this before in a government office.

Shit, I thought, do these welfare cases freak out if they get denied money or something? Do these clerks really need to hide behind a pane of glass?

I looked at the people in the welfare office. There weren't too many people in there because the place had just opened for the day, but the ones that were there looked pretty rough. One broad looked like a crack whore. Another guy—this old black dude—had this little metal cart with all of his belongings in it. He was talking to himself. He looked totally crazy.

This was, after all, a downtown Toronto welfare office, I told myself. I figured that the staff probably just wanted to be cautious. Every day, they had to deal with all kinds of street people, some of whom were serious drug addicts and had severe mental problems.

I walked over to the far side of the room and got into the line. It was a short line. The area where the staff sat was big and there were a few clerks at wickets serving people, so it moved pretty fast.

Within a few minutes, I got called up to one of the wickets. To talk to the clerk, it was like being at the subway station—you had to speak to the person through the glass.

"How can I help you?" the clerk said to me.

"I'm homeless," I said. "I'm staying next door, at Turning Point. I'm here to see if I can get a welfare cheque."

"OK. Do you have two pieces of ID with you?"

"Yeah, I do. Hold on a sec."

I took out my wallet, got out two pieces of ID, and then dropped them into the metal tray, where the glass met the counter.

The clerk took my IDs, looked at them, asked me a couple of questions, and then gave me a little piece of paper with a number written on it.

"OK, if you'll just please have a seat," the clerk said. "We'll be calling you up to the front again in a moment."

I didn't have to wait very long. In about ten minutes, I got called back up to the front.

"A worker is ready to speak with you now," the clerk told me. "Please go to cubicle number two."

On the wall, on the right-hand side of the room, next to a hallway, were two cubicles with telephones in them.

"I've got to call the social worker?" I said.

"No, all you're going to do is sit in the cubicle and pick up the phone," the clerk said. "The social worker will be on the other line."

Wow, I thought. You can't even talk to the social worker in person here. You have to talk to them over the phone.

I went over to cubicle number two. I sat down in the chair, picked up the phone and talked with the social worker.

The worker asked me a shitload of questions. When she was done, she told me how much assistance I was eligible to receive.

"Since you're not paying rent, you're only eligible to receive a basic needs allowance at this time," she said.

This was the one hundred and ninety bucks a month that buddy had told me about at the shelter.

"All right," I said.

The welfare office made a cheque out to me right there, on the spot.

When my cheque was ready, I went to the front and signed for it. Then they released it to me.

"If you cash it at the Royal Bank on Yonge and Bloor, you won't pay a service charge," the clerk told me.

"OK, thanks," I said.

I took my cheque and got the fuck out of there.

The first thing I did was go straight to the bank that welfare had told me to go to and cashed my cheque.

It was snowing when I got out of the bank, so I took the

subway down to Dundas Station, and then went into the shopping mall near the northeast corner of Yonge and Dundas.

Inside this mall, it was like an indoor strip mall. It was just a lineup of stores from one end to the other. The stores were so small that you couldn't even go into them; you just stood at the front of the store and told the clerk what item you wanted and they got it for you.

There was an Adidas outlet store in this mall. I had no intention of going shopping, but as I walked by it, I just happened to notice that they had that jacket that I'd seen at Foot Locker—the one I didn't buy because they'd wanted two hundred bucks for it.

"How much is that jacket?" I asked the clerk.

"This one?" the clerk said.

"No, the one next to it. The one that looks like it's got diamonds on it."

The clerk took the jacket off the rack. She looked at the price tag. "It's Ninety-nine, ninety-nine," she said.

A hundred bucks, I thought. *Half* price.

"OK, I'll take it," I said.

"How will you be paying?"

"Cash."

Because it wasn't a winter coat, I couldn't wear it yet.

As soon as I'd paid for the jacket, I ripped off the price tag, stuffed the jacket into my backpack and then walked on through the mall . . .

17

The money I got back from doing my taxes didn't last me very long. Even though I was staying in the shelter every night, I was spending money the way I'd been spending it when I was squeegeeing. Every day I was in Foot Locker spending at least a hundred bucks. I was also buying lots of weed. From the time I left the shelter in the morning to the time I got back there at night, I was always stoned.

Towards the end of February, the money ran out. I had to go back to squeegeeing.

I ran into Mark one morning at the shelter. I'd seen the guy here and there, at the shelter, over the previous couple of weeks, but I hadn't really talked to him.

"I'm coming with you to the corner today," I said to Mark.

"Oh, is the vacation over?" Mark said.

Mark was just joking. He knew I'd been sick with

pneumonia. He didn't know about the tax money, though, so he probably figured that I'd just been recuperating.

"Yeah," I said. "It's time to get back to the daily grind."

Mark and I walked over to Church and Bloor. It was a really cold day. It was probably around minus twenty with the wind chill. We were going through another one of those cold snaps that Toronto would get every so often.

Before Mark and I got our bucket, we walked up to the Canadian Tire and got a jug of de-icer. When we got back to Bloor Street, we went to the coffee shop, had something to eat, got our bucket and got straight to work.

Like before I'd gotten sick, it was just me and Mark at our corner. There were no other squeegee kids there.

We worked for not even an hour and then Mark told me he was taking off. I knew what this meant. He had enough for a twenty piece or whatever, and he was going to go get high.

"You're doing that shit already?" I said. "We haven't even been out here long."

"Yeah," Mark said.

I wasn't about to lecture the guy.

"All right," I said. "Whatever."

"I'll be back in an hour, OK?" Mark said.

It was clear that Mark was really falling into the drugs now. He'd become like those squeegee kids he'd criticized when I'd first met him—those guys who were just working, basically, for their next hit. When I'd first met Mark, he could at least work for four hours before going to get high. And he wasn't even doing it daily. For a week, there, after Boxing Day, we were going every day to the hotel. It seemed like Mark had really gone downhill since then, especially in the few short weeks since I'd gotten sick.

It was sad, seeing someone go down that road of drug abuse, but it hardly fazed me. I'd seen so many people fall into drugs on the carnival. I'd fallen in myself a couple of times really bad with the fucking crack, but I'd always managed to straighten myself out.

Whatever, I thought. It's Mark's life. It's his fucking problem, not mine.

Not long after Mark left, Scottie showed up. He'd heard from Mark that I'd been sick and asked how I was doing.

"Better," I said.

"I heard you were in the hospital," Scottie said.

"Yeah, I was in there for almost a week."

"Jesus. What'd you have?"

"Pneumonia. The doctor told me when I left that I'd have a permanent scar on my left lung."

The light changed. I went back to work. Scottie jumped in and worked alongside me.

We worked for about forty-five minutes, at which time Mark came back to the corner. Scottie stepped aside and let me and Mark work. He hung out with us at the corner and talked to us in between lights.

As soon as Mark had enough for another twenty piece, he took off again. Scottie jumped back in.

By noon, I'd already made about two hundred dollars. I was looking to take off. Mark hadn't come back yet, though, so I decided to just take off. I figured the days of going to the Waverly with Mark were probably long over, given his current drug use.

"Hey, Scottie, are you going to stick around here?" I said.

"Yeah, for a little while longer," Scottie said. "Why?"

"OK. Because I want to take off. If Mark doesn't come back, could you return the bucket for us?"

"Sure. No problem."

I left Church and Bloor and walked over to the Eaton Centre. The first thing I did was go into Foot Locker and buy myself some more clothes.

In a couple of weeks, the weather got warmer. It was March now. During the day it was consistently in the low pluses. We started getting some rain. Rain was like snow, though; you couldn't squeegee.

One morning, in the middle of March, Mark and I left the shelter and the ground outside was wet. It wasn't raining, but it had rained overnight.

We went to our corner. It was a cold, damp day. The sky was grey. It was gloomy outside. There were big puddles all over the place.

I was in kind of a blah mood. I didn't really feel like working. The weather sure didn't help. I was going through the motions that morning, while Mark and I worked. Even though it had rained overnight, the cars were still dirty because most of them had just come off the freeway and had dirty water splashed all over their windshields. There were lots of windows to clean.

As I was walking down the lineup on a light, I saw a car that was really dirty. It had obviously been inside a garage overnight or in underground parking because it was a lot dirtier than all the other cars out on the road. I did the windows on this car. I had time left on the light, so I went to look for another one.

The next car that I approached, the driver immediately puts his wipers on because he didn't want his windows done. I just saw this and thought, "You fucking dick."

I didn't even bother with this guy. I didn't try to be funny or get a smile out of him because I just didn't care. I wasn't into it. I didn't even want to be out there. I'd get days like this on the carnival, too, when I just didn't feel like entertaining anyone. It was like anything else. Some days, you just didn't feel like fucking working.

An hour into the workday, it started raining.

"Fuck it," Mark said. "I'm taking off."

"Yeah, me, too," I said. "I'm already not fucking into it."

Because I hadn't been trying very hard, or doing my act, I'd only made about twenty bucks.

Mark and I went our separate ways. I hung out in the malls the rest of the morning. In the afternoon, I went to the Evergreen.

At the Evergreen, I ran into Russ. "Hey, it's weird seeing you here," I said to him.

"Yeah, it's like I said, though," Russ said. "I still come by here sometimes."

Russ had this girl with him. I'd seen her around, at the Evergreen, but I'd never talked to her.

"This is my girlfriend, Jen," Russ told me.

Russ and Jen were sitting at one of the round tables. I sat down with them and ate my soup.

For a while, the three of us hung out at the table and talked. Russ's girlfriend seemed all right. She didn't really say all that much, though, so it was kind of hard to tell what she was like as a person.

After about an hour, we all got up and went outside to go have a smoke. It wasn't raining anymore. The sun had actually come out.

While the three of us were outside smoking, some cop came by and started giving us a hard time.

"You guys can't stand here like this," the cop told us.

"Why not?" Russ said.

"Because you're in the middle of the sidewalk."

Where we were standing was right next to the ventilation grate for the subway system. All along Yonge Street, there were these grates. The grate that we were standing next to wasn't in front of the Evergreen, it was more in front of the building next door to it.

"So what?" I said to the cop. "Who cares if we're in the middle of the sidewalk? We're on city property, man. We can stand wherever we want."

While the cop was standing there, I spit down the grate for the subway.

"I should charge you with spitting," the cop said to me.

"Go ahead," I said.

The cop didn't charge me. He just stood there for a couple more minutes, scanning the street, doing whatever the fuck it was that beat cops did, and then he left.

"We're going to get going now," Russ told me.

"All right," I said. "Nice meeting you, Jen." Then I turned to Russ. "I'll see you tonight, at the shelter."

Russ and his girlfriend took off down Yonge Street towards Dundas Street. I had nothing to do, so I went back inside the Evergreen and hung out there a bit longer . . .

18

Aside from a few rainy days in March, it turned out to be not too bad of a spring. There were only a few days where I couldn't work in the mornings because it was raining.

Once April hit, it became a lot warmer outside. The bugs came out. Mark told me that it was an early spring. "The bugs aren't usually out this early," he said. "They usually don't come out for another few weeks."

It was hard to clean the windows with the fucking bugs. The bug guts were like glue. So after struggling for a couple of days, Mark and I went to the Canadian Tire one morning and bought a jug of windshield washer fluid for spring and summer. This shit was pink. Mark and I used it the same way we'd used the de-icer in the winter. We had the coffee shop fill our bucket halfway with water, and then we topped it up with the washer fluid. Whatever we didn't use from the jug, we chucked.

The pink shit helped dissolve the bug guts. I was able to get the windows done way faster than with just plain water. The first window I did, the gluey crap came right off.

"This stuff works great," I said to Mark.

"Yeah," Mark said. "You don't have to apply so much pressure."

Later that morning, Scottie came by. Mark and I were both at the corner.

Scottie told us about a squeegee kid who'd gone psycho the day before, and who'd smashed out the window of somebody's car.

"Where did that happen?" Mark said.

"Right here, at this corner," Scottie said. "It happened in the afternoon."

I was never at Church and Bloor anymore in the afternoons. I'd only ever gone there at that time of day when Mark and I were going to the Waverly, which hadn't been since January, before I'd gotten sick.

Mark, apparently, had been going there regularly in the afternoons, though. Because he was taking off so much, during the day, to get high, he had to be out there all day now to make the same money.

"I was here yesterday, in the afternoon," Mark said to Scottie. "I didn't see anything like that happen."

"It happened not long after you left," Scottie said. "I came by at around four thirty. You were already gone. I was hanging out, when I saw that punker guy—you know that guy who works across the street sometimes?"

"Yeah," Mark said.

"Well, anyway, some asshole didn't want to pay him or whatever. So when the light changed, before the guy could drive away, he swung his squeegee at the guy's rear window and smashed out the glass. There must have been a cop around the corner or something because the cops were here right away. They slapped the cuffs on the guy and then shoved him into the squad car."

Even though the driver of the car had probably been an asshole, fucking up the guy's car was a bad move, I thought. It made us all look bad.

Mark didn't seem to care. "Yeah, whatever," he said. "I'm sure the guy deserved it. He just made the mistake of messing with the wrong person."

The next morning, Mark and I left the shelter and walked to the Canadian Tire. As we walked over there, Mark didn't say much. It seemed like he was pissed off about something, but he obviously didn't want to talk about it.

We got to the Canadian Tire, bought a jug of windshield washer fluid, and then walked back to Bloor Street.

At the coffee shop, while we were eating breakfast, Mark finally told me what was bothering him. "Some guy ripped me off yesterday," he said. "He was supposed to run for me to get me some dope, but he didn't come back. He just took my money and fucked off with it."

"How much did he beat you for?" I said.

"Twenty-five bucks. It's not that much, but that's not the point, you know?"

"Yeah, I know. You don't want people to hear that, and then think you're a bitch."

"Exactly. I'm telling you, Jim, if I see that guy today and he doesn't have my money, I'm going to punch him in his fucking face. Then I'm going to tell him, 'If I see you again, and you *still* don't have my money, I'm going to punch you again.'"

I didn't want to add any more fuel to the fire. I didn't say anything. I just let Mark rant.

We finished eating. Mark left a lot of food behind, on his plate. I figured his drug habit was affecting his appetite. It wasn't just his mood that day. He hadn't been eating properly as of lately. You could tell just by looking at him. His face was starting to look thinner.

We went up to the counter and got our bucket. Then we went outside and doused it with the pink wiper fluid, or "bug juice," as we called it.

We were only out there for about an hour, when some fucking motorist moved his car, suddenly, while Mark was in front of it, and nearly ran over his foot.

"I can't handle this shit today," Mark said to me when we got back to the curb. "I'm going to get out of here. I'll see you later."

19

The next morning Mark and I left the shelter and walked over to our corner to squeegee. Mark seemed to be in a better mood.

After working for about half an hour, Mark told me that he'd be back in a few minutes. "I'm just going inside to the coffee shop," he said. "I've got to take a piss."

I worked through the next light by myself. When the light changed, I went back to the corner. Mark was standing there. He had his hands in his pockets. He was grinning at me.

"Guess what?" Mark said.

"What?" I said.

"I just scored a thousand bucks."

Mark was wearing that green hoodie he wore a lot. It had a pouch at the front of it, where you could put your hands. He clearly had something stashed in there.

Mark let me take a peek at what he had in his pouch. He kind of pulled it out from one side, just enough for me to see it. It was a big stack of twenty-dollar bills.

"Where the fuck did you get that?" I said.

"That bank machine over there," Mark said.

There was a bank machine right outside of the building that the coffee shop was in. The machine was right on the street, facing the sidewalk, like in the movies. You didn't have to go in any door to use the machine. You could just walk right up to it and use it.

"I was just walking towards the building when I happened to look over and notice that the bank machine was at the screen that said, 'Would you like to perform another transaction?'" Mark said.

"OK," I said. "So, someone left their card in the machine?"

"Yeah. As soon as I saw that, I was like, 'Cool. Send it in.' I went up to the machine, pressed 'yes,' and then I took out the maximum amount of money that the machine would let me take out."

I shook my head. "That wasn't too smart," I said. "Those bank machines all have cameras on them. The cops are going to come here now. They're going to be looking for you, man."

"No they won't," Mark said. "I had my hood up. My head was down the whole time. All the cops are going to be able to see on the surveillance tape is the hood. They're not going to be able to see my face."

Mark took his squeegee out of our bucket. "All right, I'm going to take off now," he said. "I'll see you later, Jim."

I sighed. "OK," I said. "See ya."

I figured that Mark was going to score some dope and

then fall in big time. That thousand bucks wouldn't last him long. It was too bad, really, because I knew that once Mark came to his senses, he'd realize that he'd really fucked himself by ripping off that bank machine. He might have had his hood up, when he'd gone to the machine, but the cops were still going to be looking for him. It would be stupid for him to come back to Church and Bloor.

When Scottie came by later that morning, I told him about what Mark had done.

At first, Scottie thought it was a good score.

"How was it a good score?" I said. "He can't come back to this corner now."

"You said he had his hood up, though," Scottie said.

"Yeah, so?" I said. "The cops can still make out some physical description from the tape. You know, it was bad enough what that lugen did the other day, smashing out the back of that car window. Now Mark's brought even more heat on us."

"Do you really think the cops are going to come here?"

"Probably."

Surely enough, the next day, this is exactly what happened. I was at Church and Bloor by myself. It was early. I'd no sooner gotten my bucket from the coffee shop and started to work, when some cop showed up, looking for the guy who ripped off the bank machine.

The cops knew that it was one of the squeegee kids who had done this. Apparently, it was the security guard from the building that the coffee shop was in who had left his bank card in the machine the day before.

"The security guard looked at the surveillance images himself," the cop told me. "He said he recognized the guy who'd used his card. He said that it was one of the squeegee kids who normally works at this corner—some guy who's always wearing a green hoodie."

I just played dumb. "I don't know," I said. "I don't know anyone like that, man."

"You have no idea who this person is?" the cop said.

"Nope."

"You work here every day?"

"Not every day."

"Well, you're here a lot, though, right?"

"Yeah."

"OK. So, how come you don't know who did it? Don't you guys talk to each other? Don't you all hang out and stuff?"

"I don't hang out with any of these guys. I keep to myself. Anyway, I'm not here all day. I'm only ever here for a few hours at a time. I don't know what happens around here when I'm not around."

Because I wouldn't cooperate with him, the cop started hassling me even more. "You can't be doing this here," he said. "You've got to go."

"What are you talking about?" I said. "I've been working here every day since December. I've never been told by any cops that I can't do this here."

"Well, I'm telling you right now, OK? So, pack up your stuff. I want you off this corner."

"Or what, you're going to give me a ticket?"

"Do you want me to?"

"No, but if you are, then just give it to me already, and then get out of my face, and let me get back to work, so I can make some money to fucking pay it."

I knew the cop couldn't give me a ticket. I'd never heard from Mark or Scottie of anyone getting a ticket for squeegeeing. What I was doing wasn't illegal. I was at a red light. I wasn't holding up traffic, or obstructing it, in any way.

The cop turned, like he was about to leave. Suddenly, he stepped towards my bucket and kicked it over. Water spilled all over the sidewalk. It went over the curb and into the road.

"Do you feel better now?" I said to the cop. "You know, I can go into that building right over there and they'll give me a refill."

The cop looked at me with disgust. "I want you off this corner," he said. "I don't want to see you back here tomorrow, OK?"

"Yeah, whatever," I muttered.

The cop turned and walked away.

20

The cop didn't show up the next day. I didn't end up seeing him again. I wasn't out there much longer, though. Only a couple of days later, I quit squeegeeing and went to the carnival. It was about a week into April now and the shows were starting up. It was time to go back to it.

I went through the phone numbers in my wallet of the work acquaintances I had in Toronto. I called up this guy named Newfie. Newfie was an old guy who lived in Toronto. I'd met him one year on this show called Sammy's Amusements—a little show that played spots that were mostly in the Greater Toronto Area.

I had to jog the old guy's memory a little bit, but he remembered me.

"Oh, *hey*, Jimmy," Newfie said. "Long time no see."

"Yeah, how's it going?" I said.

"Ah, not bad. Health ain't so great, you know? But that's

nothing new. So, anyway, how are you doing, kid? Where are you at right now?"

"I'm in town."

"Oh, yeah?"

"Yeah, I'm in Toronto. Listen, man, I need to get working. I was thinking of working for Sammy this season. Do you know if he's got any spots lined up yet?"

"Yeah, Sammy's out already. We've already played one spot. The next one's at Vic and Danforth. Why don't you come down to the lot tomorrow? We're going to start setting up the joints."

"Vic and Danforth? Where's that?"

"It's in the east end. It's right on the Bloor-Danforth subway line. You get off at Victoria Park subway station, and then you just walk down the street. There's a plaza there, right at the intersection. That's where we're setting up, in the parking lot."

"OK, I'll just look it up on the subway map."

"There you go."

"All right, then. I'll see you tomorrow."

In the morning I left the shelter at eight o'clock and took the TTC to Victoria Park subway station. It took me about half an hour to get there.

I left the subway and walked down the street to Victoria Park and Danforth. The lot was on the southwest corner of the intersection.

I crossed the street and went over to the lot. As soon as I got there, I ran into Sammy. He remembered me right away.

"Hey, Jimmy, how's it going?" Sammy said.

"I need a hole, Sammy," I said. "You got a joint I could work in?"

"Yeah. I need someone in the smash."

The plate smash was the game where you threw baseballs at dinner plates and tried to break them. I usually worked in build-up games, or "prize every time" games, but I could work a smash. It was actually the first game I'd ever worked in, back in '92, for Conklin.

"Yeah, no problem," I said.

"OK, great," Sammy said. "We're going to be setting up the lineups in a couple of minutes."

The lineups were the joints that formed the perimeter of the midway. These always got set up first. After these were done, the show set up the joints in the centre of the midway.

We worked until five o'clock that day, setting up the joints. We finished the lineups. I had to come back the next day to help set up the centre joints.

Before I left the lot, I went to the office trailer and bought a show shirt. The shirt was just a basic t-shirt with the name of the show on the front of it, and the word "staff" written across the back. The shirt was important because not only was it my uniform, it also served as proof to the staff at Turning Point that I had a job. If I was going to work on the show, I was going to need to be able to stay out past their stupid ten o'clock curfew. I could have stayed on the lot, in a bunkhouse, but I already had such a good deal at the shelter. I got to stay there for free and get free meals. I got to live in an actual house, in a central location that was close to transit. You couldn't beat that. It was a lot better than staying in a dirty bunkhouse with no heating for fifty bucks a week.

That night, when I went back to the shelter, I had the show shirt on underneath my jacket. I let the staff see the shirt, and asked them if they could make an exception for me with regards to the curfew.

"We don't close until eleven o'clock at night," I said. "I'll be taking the TTC. Sometimes I'll be coming from all the way across town. It could take me two hours to get here."

Vadim and Andrew were both in the office area. Vadim looked at Andrew.

"Well, I'm OK with it," Andrew said

"Yeah, I think we can make an exception for you, Jim, because you have a job," Vadim said.

"Thanks," I said.

The next morning, I went back to the lot. We finished setting up the centre joints. The stock truck hadn't arrived yet by five o'clock, so the boss told everyone that we'd be flashing the joints—stocking them, in other words—the next day, before we opened. Because it was a weekday and school was in session, we couldn't open until four o'clock in the afternoon.

It didn't take me long to flash my joint the next day. Because I was in the plate smash, I only had one size stock—big pieces. I hung the stock in two rows, one on top of another, on either side of the joint. Then I was done.

At four o'clock, when we opened, it was really slow. Things didn't start to pick up until a couple of hours later.

When people finally started to walk down the midway, I called in everyone who walked by my game. To kids, I said stuff like, "We don't wash dishes here, we break 'em!" To the guys with their wives or girlfriends, I said, "If you break a plate here, you don't have to buy her a new set!" No matter what I said, though, nothing seemed to work. People would smile, giggle, or stare dumbly at me, and then just walk on by.

What the hell's wrong with these people? I thought to myself. Why do they come here if they don't want to spend any fucking money?

By the time we closed at eleven o'clock, I'd only managed to gross twenty dollars. I'd made less than minimum wage. It was probably the worst day I'd ever had on the carnival—on any show.

I went back to the shelter that night, feeling so depressed. Winston, one of the staff who usually worked the night shift, let me in. He was sitting in the office area by the entrance, doing some paperwork.

"How was work?" Winston said.

"Not so great," I said.

"Why, what happened?"

"Oh, it was just pretty dead there."

"You sound hoarse."

"Yeah, it's from yelling all night. That's what you have to do when you work in a game—call people in. I haven't done this since October. It takes me a few days to get used to it."

I said goodnight to Winston, had a smoke on the balcony, and then went to bed.

I was hoping that the weekend would be better, but it was the same bullshit as Friday night. The spot just sucked. It was a blank. The only joint that seemed to be making any money was the balloon store. I watched the guy in the balloons for a few minutes on one of my breaks. The guy was an older guy; he was really strong in the joint. I watched him get a hundred bucks off some broad in a couple of minutes and kick out a big piece of stock. This guy was working hard; he was calling people in left and right. I was working hard, too, I just had nothing to show for it in my apron.

I'd never gone out this early in the season in Ontario. The last time I'd worked for Sammy, the first spot I'd played had been in May. I had no idea that the early spots were this bad. The worst part of it all was that Victoria Park and Danforth was a ten-day spot. I was going to be stuck there, blanking out every day for another seven days.

As we were closing up on Sunday night, I talked to Newfie. He was in a centre joint, right across from me.

"This spot really sucks," I said. "I'm not making any money here, Newfie. I'm starting to get frustrated."

"I know," Newfie said. "But it's early in the season, Jimmy. It'll pick up, man. Just stick with it."

21

I decided to listen to Newfie and stick with the show. If I was going to survive, though, I had to find a way to supplement my income until the spots got better.

On Monday morning, I ran into Russ as I was leaving the shelter. Russ had told me once that he could get me any kind of drugs I wanted, so I asked him, as soon as we were out on the street, if he could get me an ounce of weed.

"Yeah, I can get you an ounce of weed," Russ said. "I told you that. I can get you any kind of drugs you want."

"OK," I said. "When can you get it for me?"

"I can get it for you right now."

"Wow. OK. Well, I don't have the money up front. That's why I need it. Could you front me and I'll pay you back?"

"Yeah, that's fine. Pay me back when you get rid of it."

"OK. How much do you want for it?"

"Two hundred."

My plan was to start selling an ounce of weed every day in front of the Evergreen. I didn't really want to sell drugs—I'd done it in Edmonton. It was the reason I'd left town with the show in the first place. But I needed money and selling weed was something that I knew how to do. With all the people coming by that place on a daily basis, buying dime bags, I figured I'd be able to get rid of an ounce a day easily. It would keep me going until the spots picked up.

Russ took off right away to get the weed. We met up two hours later at the Second Cup by the Evergreen.

"Let's go to the park across the street," Russ said.

We jaywalked across Yonge Street, walked down Yonge to the path on the side of College Park, and then followed the path to Barbara Ann Scott Park.

We went right to the back of the park. Russ gave me the weed. I put it in my backpack.

"Want to go get a coffee?" Russ said.

"Sure," I said.

We walked back over to the Second Cup.

We hung out for a while, drank our coffees, and then Russ told me that he had to go do some stuff.

"All right," I said. "I'll see you later."

"Have a good one," Russ said.

After Russ took off, I went and found a head shop. I bought a digital scale for about thirty bucks and some baggies. Then I headed over to the Evergreen.

On my way over there, I passed a fast food joint. I went inside, went into the bathroom, and then made up ten dime bags really quickly, in one of the stalls. To do this, I sat on the toilet, put my scale on my lap, put some weed in a bag, and then put the bag on the scale. The bag itself had some weight to it, so after subtracting the weight of the bag, each bag had to weigh 0.7 grams. That was the proper count for a dime. I was going to sell each dime bag for ten bucks. Out of an ounce, I got forty dimes, so I was making four hundred bucks.

The weed was fluffy. It looked really big in the bag. It looked like a full gram, even though it was only 0.7 grams.

When I got to the Evergreen, it was around eleven thirty in the morning. There were no dealers out there yet. At any given time during the day, there were usually three or four dealers out there, but they didn't start hanging out there until at least noon.

Within a couple of minutes, someone came up to me. It was a guy in his late teens or early twenties. He looked like the college type—clean-cut, backpack, glasses. I figured he went to Ryerson College.

"Hey, do you know where I can get some weed?" the guy asked me.

"Yeah, I've got some," I said. "How much do you want?"

"I've got ten bucks."

The guy gave me ten dollars. I gave him one dime bag. Then the guy took off.

Over the next half hour, I sold another four dimes. Yonge Street was busy. People were coming by at a steady rate, looking for weed. It seemed like every five or six minutes, I was making a sale. Most people just bought a single dime.

The action that I was getting was about what I'd expected. I found it pretty nerve-wracking, though, once I was out there, in front of the Evergreen, hustling weed. I'd never hustled drugs on the street before. When I'd sold weed in Edmonton, I'd started off selling only to people that I knew, and then I'd moved up in weight. The only good thing about the Evergreen was the set-up. The spot where I was standing was sunk back a few feet from the rest of the storefronts on Yonge Street, which meant that a cop walking along Yonge couldn't see me from down the street. I still had to be aware of my surroundings, of course, but I didn't have to look over my shoulder constantly. I only had to really pay attention to what was going on directly across the street from me.

At a quarter after twelve, another dealer showed up.

"Hey, Craig," I said.

"Hey, Jim," Craig said. "You're out here now?"

"Yeah," I said.

"Cool. What are you selling?"

"Just weed," I said.

Craig nodded. "All right," he said. "Just wondering."

In a couple of minutes, another customer came by—a girl in her twenties. She went to Craig because she knew him. Basically, that was the way it worked in front of the Evergreen, or anywhere else I'd ever bought drugs, where there were multiple dealers hanging out, selling— whichever dealer the customer approached is the one that got the sale. If a customer already knew a certain dealer, then, of course, they'd approach that dealer.

In about an hour, I'd gotten rid of the ten dime bags I'd made up. Just as I was taking off to go find a bathroom, so I could make up ten more, one of the staff at the Evergreen showed up.

I'd never talked to this particular staff member before when I was at the Evergreen, but she seemed to recognize me. How could she not? I was there all the time, hanging out and eating the five-cent soup.

"Hello," the broad said to me, as she put her key in the door.

"Hey," I said. Then I took off to go find a bathroom.

Not long after the Evergreen opened up at one o'clock, two more dealers showed up. Right away, they wanted to know what I was selling.

"Just weed," I said.

"All right," the dealers said.

At a quarter after two, it was time to go to the show. I had to be there at three o'clock to open up my joint at four. I'd already sold almost thirty dimes.

I left the Evergreen, walked up to Carlton Street, and then went into the subway.

That night, I blanked out again on the show. It was two miserable hours before I got even one customer. It was so dead there that we closed early. At ten thirty, I'd already locked up my joint and was on my way out of there.

I went back to the Evergreen to sell the rest of my weed. It was late, but Yonge Street was still really busy. People were constantly walking by, coming out of restaurants and bars. I figured that the traffic on a street like that probably didn't start to thin out until at least two o'clock in the morning, when the bars closed.

By around midnight, I'd sold out of dimes. I kept one for myself, so I could smoke a joint in the morning, and then I went back to the shelter.

I had my show shirt on underneath my jacket. When I got to the shelter, I unzipped my jacket so that the shirt would be visible to the staff.

"I'm just going to go have a smoke," I said to Winston, when I got in the door.

"Yeah, no problem," Winston said.

I went out onto the balcony and had a smoke. While I was out there, I counted my money. There was a surveillance camera out there, so I made sure to stand with my back to it.

I quickly counted up three hundred and ninety dollars. I'd sold thirty-nine dime bags—forty, minus the one I'd kept for myself.

OK, I thought. That checks out.

I put the money back in my pocket. Then I finished my smoke, went back inside, and went to bed.

22

After selling weed for a few days, I decided to quit the show. Even though I'd only intended on selling weed until the spots got better, I was making so much money selling dimes, with the constant stream of people coming by the Evergreen, that it just didn't make sense to stick it out on the carnival. I thought, "Why waste my time?"

I didn't have any long-term plans or anything. I was just looking to make some quick money and to support myself. Selling weed was obviously the way to do it because I didn't want to go back to squeegeeing. I was done with that shit. I'd done it when I'd needed to do it, but selling weed was so much easier. And anyway, I kind of felt that what Mark had done had ruined things at Church and Bloor. I didn't want to have to deal with that asshole cop again. I had no idea what the hell had even happened to Mark. I hadn't seen him back at Turning Point after that day.

A couple of days before the weekend, I told the boss that I was quitting. He didn't seem to really care. He paid me for the spot, and then I walked out of there. I made sure to hang onto my show shirt.

I went to the Evergreen after work that night, got rid of my weed, and then went back to the shelter.

"Hey, Jim, how was work?" Winston asked me when I walked in the door.

"It was all right," I said.

As far as the shelter staff knew, I still had the job on the show, and that was how I wanted things to stay. That job was my alibi; my excuse to stay out late. All I had to do was wear my show shirt back to the shelter every night, and I could continue to sell weed and come back there at twelve, one o'clock in the morning.

The day after I quit the show, I was leaving the shelter with Russ in the morning, when I noticed that he had all his stuff with him.

"Why do you have all your stuff with you today?" I said.

"Because," Russ said, "I'm leaving."

"*Leaving*?"

"Yeah. You know Jen, that girl I've been seeing?"

"Yeah."

"We got a place together. We're moving in today."

I was stunned. Russ had never mentioned to me that he was looking for an apartment. But, then again, Russ never told me much about his personal life. We just didn't talk about that stuff.

This news couldn't have come at a worse time for me. Right away, I started to worry about how the hell I was going to get my weed. I trusted Russ. I knew that if I was dealing with him, shit would get done. I knew that he wasn't going to set me up to get robbed or some bullshit like that. He was a decent person. I didn't know anyone else like that on the street.

Russ noticed the look on my face. He started to laugh. "Relax," he said. "I'm not going far, Jim. I can still get you weed, if you want. You can come to my place in the mornings to pick it up. I'll actually be closer to my weed guy now, where I'm moving to."

"Where are you moving to?"

"You know where Parkdale is?"

I knew exactly where Parkdale was. It was a neighbourhood right by the Exhibition grounds. People called it "Crackdale" because it was an area that was notorious for drugs and hookers. Whenever I was in Toronto, playing the Canadian National Exhibition with Conklin, I'd go there to score dope. At night, after work, I'd leave through the Dufferin Gate, and then I'd go to Lansdowne and Queen.

"Yeah, I know where Parkdale is," I said.

"All right," Russ said. "Well, my place is right before you get to Parkdale. If you're downtown and you're heading west along Queen, it's right before you get to Dufferin. It's on the south side of Queen."

Russ gave me his street address. Then he told me what his building looked like. It was a low-rise building, three storeys high.

"I don't have a phone number for you yet," Russ said. "We're getting our phone hooked up today. Tomorrow, if you want an ounce, you've got to come down to my place and buzz me, OK? I'm in unit 301."

"All right," I said. "I'll do that. Thanks."

"Do you want me to get you an ounce right now?"

"Yeah."

I gave Russ the cash.

"OK, I'll go get it right now," Russ said. "See you later, at the Second Cup."

Later that day, while I was out in front of the Evergreen, hustling dimes, one of the dealers there, Craig, came up to me.

"Hey, I can't get a hold of my dealer," Craig said. "I'm out of dimes. Could you front me some? I'll pay you back as soon as I sell them."

I wasn't going to front this guy. I didn't trust him enough to do that.

"I'll tell you what," I said. "I'll give you a deal."

I pulled a dime out of my pocket. I opened my hand a little, so that Craig could take a look at it.

"I'll sell you five of these fat-ass dimes for thirty-five bucks," I said.

Craig was impressed by the count in the bag. "Wow, that's a pretty fat-assed dime," he said. "Yeah, OK. Give me five of those, then."

Craig gave me thirty-five bucks. I gave him the five dimes.

Even though it was less profit for me, selling five dimes for thirty-five bucks, when I could have gotten fifty bucks for them, I gave Craig this deal because my intention was to get some of these guys, who hustled weed in front of the Evergreen, to start coming to me whenever they needed more dimes, instead of going to whoever it was that they were getting their weed from. Once I had a few of these guys buying dimes off me, I wouldn't have to stand out there anymore, hustling them myself. That was my plan. I really couldn't stand being out there, I realized. I just felt so paranoid. When you're a drug dealer, and you're out on the street like that, you're like a sitting duck for the cops. Let these younger guys take the risk, I thought.

About an hour after I'd given Craig this deal, this guy named Danzig showed up. He was around my age—maybe a year or two older. He had a slim build and was about average height. With him was this other guy, who was about six feet tall and almost two hundred pounds. This guy's name was Moose.

Now, it was just common sense from the street that the big guy, Moose, was obviously Danzig's muscle. I'd had muscle, too, when I was in Edmonton, selling weed because I was dealing in quantity. So I understood the guy's function right away.

Because we were all in that little corner, where all the dealers stood, I was able to hear the conversation that Danzig had with the two dealers that were out there, selling weed with me.

Basically, what Danzig wanted to know was if they wanted more dimes. This was the guy who was supplying these guys, obviously; the guy whose business I was trying to cut into.

The one dealer needed to re-up.

"What about you?" Danzig said to Craig.

"Nah, I'm good," Craig said.

Danzig and Moose hung out in front of the Evergreen for a while. In between drug deals, Danzig, Craig, the other dealer who was out there, and I all stood around and talked. We didn't talk about anything in particular; we just kind of stood there, shooting the shit.

At five o'clock the Evergreen closed for the night. The staff came out, locked the door, and then they left.

Suddenly, these two teenage girls showed up. They were all trashed. They were drinking on the street and trying to start shit with people.

Some random person walked by the Evergreen suddenly. "What are *you* looking at, bitch?" one of the girls yelled.

I'd never hung out in front of the Evergreen before while the place was closed. I realized that this was when all the street riffraff came by the place to hang out. These people didn't need to be in front of the Evergreen. They had no business to conduct there. They just had nothing better to do and wanted to hang out in the street.

At some point, these two girls chased another girl down Yonge Street and beat the shit out of her. Then they ganged up on some poor guy. Nobody in front of the Evergreen did anything about it. The other dealers and I just hid in our little corner, watched this stupid shit and laughed. It was entertaining in a trashy sort of way.

"Sometimes I'll come down here just to watch the escapades," Danzig told me.

"Yeah, these people are morons," I said. "It's like watching Jerry Springer."

23

Just as I'd figured, the word got around. The next day another dealer approached me, asking me if I'd sell him some dimes.

"How many do you want?" I said.

"Give me five," the guy said. "I want that same deal you gave Craig, though—five for thirty-five bucks."

Later that day, in the evening, another dealer approached me. This guy only ever sold weed in the evenings. With these dealers, it was almost like they worked in shifts. When the guys who sold in the evening showed up, the afternoon guys left.

This guy had heard about the deal I'd given Craig and he wanted the same deal, too.

"Sure," I said.

I gave the guy five dimes. The guy gave me thirty-five bucks.

"Come back when you want more dimes," I said.

That night, by around eight o'clock, I'd sold out of weed. In order to keep up with demand, the next morning when I left the shelter, I called Russ at the payphone and asked him if he could get me two ounces.

"I can get you that for four hundred," Russ said.

"OK," I said. "I've got that on me."

"All right. I'll go get it right now."

"You don't need the money up front?"

"No, I can cover it. When you get down here, you can pay me back."

"OK, thanks. I'll see you soon."

I hung up the phone and then went into Wellesley subway station. I took a southbound train to Queen Station, and then took the streetcar along Queen Street to Russ's place. The traffic on Queen was terrible. The streetcar was slow as shit. It took me forever to get there.

As soon as I picked up the two ounces from Russ, I took the TTC to the Eaton Centre, and then went to the bathroom near the Dundas Street entrance of the mall. The bathrooms were on the lower level, by the escalator.

I went to this bathroom specifically because it was the biggest one in the mall. It had about thirty stalls. A bigger bathroom had more ventilation than a smaller one, meaning the weed would be harder to smell. This was important because I was going to sit there, in that bathroom, and dime up the entire two ounces of weed, all in one shot. In order to be able to give out deals, I needed to have all of my weed dimed up. I couldn't be running to bathrooms anymore, making up ten dimes at a time.

As soon as I had my weed dimed up, I left the mall and walked over to the Evergreen . . .

That day, a couple more dealers approached me, asking for dimes—a guy in the afternoon, and a girl in the evening. I kept re-investing my money and moving up in weight to keep up with demand, and within a couple of days, I asked Russ if he could get me four ounces, or a quarter pound, of weed.

At first, Russ was surprised that I wanted that much. "Really?" he said. "You can get rid of that much in a day?"

"Yeah," I said. "I'm not hustling it all myself, though. I've got a bunch of street dealers buying dimes off me, now, in front of the Evergreen."

"Oh, OK."

"Yeah, they're working for me, basically. They're helping me get rid of it."

"That's smart."

"Fuckin'-A. These guys aren't even going to their regular dealers anymore. All day, they're just coming to me."

"OK. Well, I can get you a QP right now. I'll only charge you six."

Six hundred bucks for a quarter pound was a better deal than what Russ had been charging me for three ounces. Like with anything else, the bigger the quantity you bought, the less you paid for it. It was always cheaper to buy quantity. Russ was obviously getting it for less than six hundred and charging me a little more to make his end for being the middle man.

As always, Russ didn't need the money up front. He immediately ran out and got the weed for me, so that by the time I got to his place, he already had it. I didn't have to wait. I never went up to Russ's apartment to do these drug deals with him. He always met me on the street, outside of his building.

"I don't like doing business in my place," Russ told me.

"I get it," I said. "Don't shit where you sleep, right?"

"Yeah."

"That's why I like dealing with you, Russ. You're cautious."

Russ laughed.

Russ and I hung out for a few minutes. Then he took off to go do whatever he had to do that day.

"OK, have a good one," Russ said.

"You, too," I said.

Later that day, while I was standing in front of the Evergreen, one of the dealers came up to me. "These counts you're giving me are so good that I've been chopping the dimes in half and selling each one as two dimes," he told me.

"That's fine," I said. "I don't care what you do, man. They're proper counts, though. They're 0.7 grams. The weed's just fluffy. It looks like one gram when it's in the bag."

I really didn't care what these guys did, honestly. If they were cutting their dimes in half, though, they were making some pretty decent profit margins. Normally, these guys would buy a handful of dimes at ten bucks a dime, take a little bit of weed out of each one and make up an extra bag. That was how they made their end. Or sometimes their dealer would give them a free bag on every ten bags or something. Because I was giving these guys such good counts, they could literally buy five dimes and sell them as ten. They were investing thirty-five bucks and turning it into a hundred bucks, in other words. They were almost tripling their money. That wasn't too bad for a sixteen-year-old street kid, nickel and diming it out on the street.

Once I got to the quarter pound level, I just stuck at that level. A quarter pound was a lot of dimes. It was one hundred and sixty dimes. I had to make sure that I could sell it all in one day. I didn't want to bring any of it back with me to the shelter at night. The whole time I'd been at the shelter, I'd never brought more than a joint or two back there at night. A lot of weed smelled a lot. It seeped through the plastic bag.

Once I had a handful of dealers buying from me, I didn't have to hustle dimes anymore to the general public. I could get rid of the entire quarter pound just by selling to these other dealers.

The next morning, after picking up a quarter pound, I went out and bought a cell phone. I needed it, now, to be in touch with these guys, since I wasn't going to be standing in front of the Evergreen anymore.

At the store, the salesclerk showed me a Nokia phone. There was nothing that flipped out at the bottom of this phone, it was just one solid piece. It had an antenna that pulled out.

"It comes with a headphone set," the salesclerk told me.

The headphone set had one headphone. It was a single earpiece with a mic.

"Have you ever had a phone like this?" the salesclerk asked me.

"No," I said. "I had a cell phone back in Edmonton about five years ago, but it was nothing like this one. It was way bulkier."

"Technology—it changes pretty fast, doesn't it?"

"Yeah, no kidding."

I paid cash for the phone. I'm sure the salesclerk knew that I was a drug dealer or something. It wasn't like I'd come in there, wearing a business suit and had paid with a credit card. The average person didn't carry around a cell phone. If you had one, you were probably either a business man or a drug dealer.

The salesclerk activated the phone for me. Then I left the store. I went straight to the Eaton Centre, made up all of my dime bags in the bathroom, and then went to the Evergreen.

That day, I hung out in front of the Evergreen, giving my cell phone number out to all of the dealers that I dealt with on a regular basis. "When you want more dimes, if I'm not here, hanging out, just call me on my cell," I told them.

The next day I hung out in front of the Evergreen again, until I'd met with all the dealers. Once they all had my number, I stopped hanging out there.

When the first dealer called me, asking for more dimes, I told him to meet me around the corner from the Evergreen, on the Ryerson College campus.

"OK," the guy said. "Where, exactly?"

"On Gerrard, two blocks east of Yonge, you'll see an interlocking brick path that leads to the campus," I said.

"Yeah, I know where that is," the guy said.

"OK. Let's meet underneath that pedway thing that connects the two buildings."

"All right. Are you going to be there right away?"

"I'll be there in fifteen minutes."

I thought this was a perfect spot to meet with these dealers. It was close to the Evergreen and it wasn't too much in plain sight. The area underneath the pedway was set back quite a ways from Gerrard Street.

I got to Ryerson in under fifteen minutes. Unlike most drug dealers, I made sure to be prompt with these guys. I didn't want them to have to wait for me. I wanted their business. I didn't want them going to someone else because they got sick of waiting around for me.

In a couple of minutes, the guy showed up. I sold him five dimes.

"Call me when you're out," I said.

"All right," the dealer said.

"We'll always meet here, OK? That way we don't have to talk about where we're going to meet all the time, over the phone."

24

It was taking me so long to get to Russ's place in the morning, with all the traffic on Queen Street, that a few days after buying the cell phone, I decided to get a pair of rollerblades. I'd be able to get to Russ's faster, I figured. I'd also be able to get to Ryerson faster to meet with the dealers.

I went to a sporting goods store in the Eaton Centre one afternoon. "What's your top-of-the-line rollerblade?" I asked the salesclerk.

I'd never owned a pair of rollerblades before. I didn't know any of the brands. All I knew was that I wanted something good. I was going to be wearing these things all day, seven days a week. I had the money. I didn't care if I had to shell out a few hundred bucks for them.

"What kind of skating are you going to be doing?" the salesclerk asked me.

"What do you mean?" I said.

"Street skating? Vert skating?"

"I don't know," I said. "I just need something that can get me around the city every day; something that can take a lot of daily wear."

The store had a huge wall full of rollerblades. While I was talking to the salesclerk, one of them caught my eye.

"Hey, what about those ones?" I said.

"The K2s?" the salesclerk said.

"Yeah, the blue and grey ones."

The boot part of the skate was blue and grey. It looked like an actual running shoe. The rest of the skate was black. It had four small wheels on it.

I looked at the price on the wall. They wanted almost three hundred and fifty bucks for these things.

"Those ones would definitely be considered 'top-of-the-line,'" the salesclerk said.

"All right," I said. "Do you have them in a nine?"

"I think I've got a nine back there," the salesclerk said. "Hold on, I'll go check."

The salesclerk went into the back room for a minute. He came back with a pair of size nines. I put them on, laced them up, and then went for a little skate around the store.

"So, how do they feel?" the salesclerk said.

"They're pretty comfortable," I said.

"Yeah, that's because of the soft boot construction. You probably notice that they're also really light-weight."

"Yeah, they do feel light on my feet."

"Did you want to try on something else?"

"No, these are good. I'll take these."

The salesclerk offered to ring up the purchase for me, but I wasn't done shopping yet.

Before I went to the cash, I went to the aisle where they had all of the accessories for bicycles and inline skates. I got two full-sized water bottles and a pair of wrist guards.

The whole point of the water bottles was so that I had a place to put my weed. The water bottles had carabiners on them so that you could clip them to your belt loops. I was going to carry these things around all day, one on each hip, like a rollerblader. I figured I'd blend right in. It was almost May. There were lots of people rollerblading around the city.

The reason I wanted the wrist guards was so that if anyone ever got in my face, I could smash them with that hard piece of plastic that covers the heel of your hand, and then make a quick getaway. I had no muscle out there, on the street. I had to think about these things.

I left the store, and then went into the first bathroom that I came to in the mall. I went into one of the stalls and put half of the dime bags I had on me into one of the water bottles, and the other half into the other one. I screwed the lids on tightly, and then hooked each water bottle to one of my belt loops.

I'd no sooner gotten outside the mall, and put on my rollerblades, when my phone started to ring. It was one of the dealers.

"Hey, Jim, can I get another five off you?" the dealer asked me.

"OK, I'll be there in two minutes," I said.

I hung up the phone and skated over to Ryerson. Even though I'd never been on rollerblades before, I had no trouble getting over there. I was a good skater. I'd been on hockey skates my whole time growing up in Edmonton. It just felt a little weird, stopping, at first. I had to keep reminding myself that I had wheels under my feet, not actual blades. If I made a hockey stop, I'd fall right over.

"Whoa, are those K2s?" the dealer asked me when I got to Ryerson.

"Yeah," I said.

"When did you get those?"

"Today."

The dealer started to tell me about how he had K2s, too, and how he wanted to get new ones. He went to skate parks and did flips and tricks on these things, apparently.

I could care less about any of this crap. These skates were just a means of transportation for me; a way to get around town.

I quickly unscrewed the lid off of one of the water bottles and gave the guy five dime bags. "Call me when you want more, OK?" I said. "I can get here really fast now."

"OK," the dealer said.

All day I just cruised around on my rollerblades and met with the dealers at Ryerson, whenever they called. I was able to get there really fast now. They'd call, and in about five to ten minutes, I'd be there.

The next morning, I left the shelter, put on my rollerblades, and then skated over to Russ's place. When I got down to Queen Street, the traffic, as usual, was terrible. I jumped onto the sidewalk, skated past the gridlock, and then got back onto the street and continued along Queen.

I got to Russ's place a lot faster than I'd ever gotten there on the streetcar.

"What's with the get-up?" Russ said when he saw me.

I quickly explained to Russ the purpose of the rollerblades, water bottles, and wrist guards.

"OK," Russ said. "For a second I thought you'd turned

into one of those fitness nuts or something. I just saw the water bottles and I was like, oh, my god . . ."

"Oh, slow down," I said.

Russ and I took care of business. We hung out for a bit afterwards. Then I skated over to the Eaton Centre. I went into the big bathroom and dimed up all of my weed. I put two ounces' worth, or eighty dime bags, into one water bottle and the rest into the other one.

Later that day, in the evening, I decided to hang out for a while in front of the Evergreen. I didn't have to do this, of course, but I was bored. I didn't feel like rollerblading. I'd skated around all day and I was tired. I wanted to take a break.

While I was hanging out there, watching the street escapades, some guy came up to me. He was a young guy. He wanted a couple of dimes, but he didn't have any cash on him. "If you give me a couple of dimes, I'll get you any pair of shoes you want," he said.

I really didn't need any more shoes, but I figured, why not? This guy's going to get me any pair I want. I can upgrade from what I've got.

I went with the guy to a shoe store right on Yonge Street. The place was near the Evergreen, but it was across the street, and a little further down Yonge, by the Swiss Chalet.

I went into the store, even though I had rollerblades on. I was only going to be in there for two seconds; I knew the store owners weren't going to say anything to me. This was a little store. They just wanted the business.

At the front of the store, I saw these brand new Adidas running shoes. I turned to the guy. "I want those ones," I said.

"Which ones?" the guy said.

"The Adidas."

"OK. All right."

I left the store and skated back to the Evergreen. A couple of minutes later, the guy showed up. He had the shoes. He'd paid for them, obviously, with a stolen credit card or something.

The guy gave me the shoes and I gave him two dimes of weed. Then he took off.

Later that night, when I got back to the shelter, I went onto the balcony to have a smoke and to count my money. I'd been doing this every single night since I'd started selling weed.

As soon as I got onto the balcony, I lit up a smoke, turned away from the surveillance camera, and with the cigarette hanging from my lips, I quickly counted what I'd grossed that day.

Since I'd started selling a quarter pound a day, the money was really starting to add up. I wasn't buying clothes at Foot Locker anymore. I was actually saving my money.

As I was standing on the balcony with all this cash in my hand, I heard a noise, suddenly. I turned my head, just as the door opened and Winston walked out onto the balcony.

I felt like a deer caught in the headlights. I needed to come up with an explanation for how I had so much money on me. "It's my pay from the carnival," I told Winston. "I haven't put any of it in the bank yet."

Winston looked at the huge wad of bills in my hand. Then he looked at me. "If you've made all that on the carnival in a couple of weeks, then you make too much money to stay here," he said. "You make more than the staff here, Jim."

I exhaled, and then looked at the ground. I knew the jig was up.

"I'm sorry," Winston said, "but this is going to have to be your last night here, OK? In the morning, you're going to have to empty your locker and go."

There was nothing I could say. I'd been caught red-handed.

"All right," I said. "I understand."

Winston went back inside.

I stood on the balcony for a couple more minutes. Then I went inside, too, and went to bed.

As I was lying in bed, trying to drift off, I stared up at the ceiling and thought about what had just happened. It was odd that Winston had come out onto the balcony like that, I thought. What I found even more odd was the fact that he hadn't even looked all that shocked. It was as if he'd been expecting to walk out there and find me counting my money. It was as if he'd gone out there for the sole purpose of catching me in the act.

I'd always been careful around the surveillance camera on the balcony. I'd always made sure to never be in view of it when I was out there, counting my money. I wondered how the staff had figured out what I'd been doing out there every night.

After thinking about it for a while, I basically came to the conclusion that the staff had probably looked at the surveillance tapes a few times and noticed that I was always out of view, with my back to the camera. They'd probably grown suspicious of me after a while and thought that if they walked out there, suddenly, they'd catch me doing whatever it was that I was doing.

In the end, though, it didn't really matter.

I guess I'm just going to have to find another place to live, I told myself.

25

I didn't really care that I was getting kicked out of Turning Point. It actually couldn't have happened to me at a better time. I was making lots of money, selling weed. I could afford to stay in a hotel.

My plan was to get a room at the Waverly. The next morning, while I was cleaning out my locker at the shelter, however, I found out about an even cheaper place that was close to the Evergreen. An acquaintance of mine at the shelter told me about it.

"It's a hospital residence," the guy said. "It's a place where people stay when they're in town, visiting relatives in the hospital. Anyone can get a room there, though. It's not that expensive. It's a lot cheaper than a hotel."

"Where is it, exactly?" I said.

"It's on Gerrard, in between Bay and University. It's right by SickKids and Toronto General."

I left the shelter with my big duffle bag and walked over to Bay and Gerrard. I found the hospital residence. It was a big building, about twenty storeys tall. It was about a block west of Bay Street, on Gerrard Street West.

I walked into the building. The lobby had a front desk like in a hotel.

I went up to the desk. "I want to get a room here," I said to the clerk.

The room was about thirty dollars. It was a very basic room, I was told. "There are no bathrooms inside the rooms here," the clerk told me. "If you need to use the toilet or shower, you have to use the community men's room down the hall from your room."

"That's fine," I said.

I paid for the room. The clerk gave me the key, and then directed me to the elevators. It was such a big building that there were three of them.

"Just so you know, the residence is only on certain floors of this building," the clerk said. "The first and second floors are a physical rehab with nurses. It's for people who've just gotten out of the hospital and who still need more care."

In the lobby were people in wheelchairs and on crutches. I figured that this was the case.

I took the elevator up to my room, on the tenth floor. Right outside of the elevators, when I got off on the tenth floor, was a lounge area. It had cushioned seating all around it and a small TV, hanging from the ceiling.

There were two hallways, one on either side of the lounge area. I walked down the hall to my room, put my key in the door, and then went inside.

It really was a basic room. It was really small. It was about the size of an average-sized bedroom in a house. All it had in it was a bed, desk, dresser, and a little closet. It didn't even have a TV.

All in all, it wasn't too bad of a deal, though, I thought. The place was cheap and it was literally right down the street from where I sold my weed. I wasn't going to be hanging out in the room much anyway. I just needed a place to sleep and to have somewhere to put my stuff.

I put my duffle bag on the bed, grabbed my rollerblades, and then left.

As soon as I got outside the building, I sat down on the steps outside and put my rollerblades on. Then I called up Russ.

"Sorry I'm calling so late today," I told Russ. "I ran into some trouble."

"What happened?" Russ said.

"Fucking Turning Point, man. They kicked me out. I had to pack up all my shit this morning and find another place to live."

"Did you find somewhere?"

"Yeah, yeah. It's fine. I'm good."

"So, what happened?"

"Ah, I got caught counting my money."

Russ laughed.

"Yeah, I was on the balcony last night," I said. "Winston walked out there suddenly and I had a few grand right in my fucking hand."

"Did he ask you why you had so much money?"

"No. He just said I had to leave."

"So, you want a QP?"

"Yeah, I'm on my way over."

"All right. See you soon."

After I picked up the weed from Russ, I went back to my room to make up the dime bags. Because the front desk had a key to my room, I was paranoid of the cleaning staff or somebody trying to come in there suddenly. What I decided to do was make up the dime bags inside the desk drawer. The desk was really close to the bed. I was able to sit on the edge of the bed with the desk drawer pulled out, and work inside of the drawer. That way, if somebody came into the room, suddenly, I could hide everything quickly by simply pushing the drawer closed.

I dimed up the quarter pound, and then left the room. As soon as I got outside, one of the dealers called me.

"Hey, I just tried to call you a minute ago," the dealer said. "You didn't answer your phone."

"Sorry, I didn't even hear it ring," I said.

"Well, anyway, I need five. How soon can you be here?"

"I can be there in a minute."

"Really?"

"Yeah, I'm just up the street."

I hung up the phone, and then skated down Gerrard Street to Ryerson College. I met with the dealer and sold him five dimes of weed.

Before I took off, I told the dealer that I was staying at the hospital residence. "Just so you know, if I'm in the elevator or something, I might not have reception on my phone," I said.

"Oh, OK," the guy said.

"So, if I don't answer, just wait a minute, and then call me back."

The day after I got the room at the hospital residence, I went to an army surplus store on Yonge Street, a couple of doors down from the Evergreen, and bought an extendable bat. It was the kind of bat that the cops carried. It was about a foot long and when you flicked it out, the thing popped open. It cost about fifty bucks.

I wasn't paranoid or anything, living at the hospital residence, but the place didn't have much security. It wasn't like at Turning Point, where the staff had to buzz you in. Here, anyone could walk inside and go up in the elevator to my floor. I felt it was necessary to get some home protection, in the same way that a person would get a baseball bat for their apartment or something.

Within a couple of days, I started to carry the bat around with me, on my person. I realized that it fit sideways, across my three back belt loops. I carried it around with enough sticking out on the one side so that I could grab it, if necessary, and whip it out. I figured that it was better protection than wrist guards. To smash someone with a wrist guard, they had to be within pretty close range.

It was around this time that I also got a bank account. I had way too much money to keep carrying it around on me, in my pocket. I couldn't leave it in my room, either, at the hospital residence because it wasn't secure. The cleaning staff came in there. There was nowhere to stash it. The only safe place that I could put it was in the bank.

I went into a TD bank one afternoon and opened a chequing account. I set up the account so that I could withdraw up to a thousand dollars a day from the bank machine. Because I still had the P.O. Box—I'd kept it going at the end of the three-month rental period—I had a mailing address to receive the bank card.

"We'll send it to your P.O. Box," the bank clerk told me. "When you receive your card in the mail, you'll need to activate it by calling the toll-free number on the back of the card."

"How long do you think it'll take for me to get the card in the mail?" I said.

"You should receive it within seven to ten business days."

Before I left the bank that day, I deposited all of my money into my chequing account. Going forward, I was going to carry as little money on me as possible.

I realized that if I'd been smarter, I would have gotten a bank account as soon as I'd started selling lots of weed. I wouldn't have gotten kicked out of Turning Point, had I done this, because I wouldn't have had all that money on me that night, on the balcony. On the seventh of May, when I turned twenty-two, I would have been kicked out of there anyway, but I could have stayed there until then. It would have been worth it, too. At Turning Point, I had no rent to pay.

In about a week, I got my bank card in the mail. That night, I dropped everything I'd grossed that day into the bank machine before going back to the hospital residence. There were TD banks all over the downtown core, so I just deposited it into the first one I ran into. All I brought back to my room with me that night were some loonies and toonies, and a few dimes of weed.

The next morning, I stopped at the bank again and withdrew the six hundred dollars I needed to pick up a quarter pound of weed. I put it in my pocket, and then skated over to Russ's place . . .

26

For a while, not much happened. Every day I just cruised around all day on my rollerblades and met the dealers at Ryerson whenever they called. One day rolled into the next. Before I knew it, it was the middle of June.

In mid-June, I started to think about my long-term plans. The whole time I'd been in Toronto, I'd never had any real plans. I'd just been trying to get by. Now that I had some money saved, I was starting to think about what I wanted to do with myself in the near future.

I knew that I didn't want to stay in Toronto and keep selling weed for months and months on end. In the drug-dealing game, you got in, made your money fast, and then you got the fuck out before you had a chance to get busted. I'd never intended on selling weed over the long-term. I'd just done it to make some quick money. Now that I had money in the bank, it was time to think about getting out.

As odd as it sounds, I thought about going back to work for Conklin. In mid-August, they'd be back in town to play the Canadian National Exhibition. I figured I could go to the lot during set-up, get a hole, work for Greg Melnik again, and then rob him blind, out of the apron. It would be compensation for him ditching my ass and leaving me stranded in the United States.

My plan was to play the CNE, and then to finish the rest of the season with Conklin. I'd get a free ride with the show to Miami, and then I'd sit on the beach and do fuck all for the winter because I'd have money saved and I wouldn't have to work. I could have a real vacation.

You deserve one, I told myself. You've been through a lot since October.

A couple of days after I'd decided all of this, I had an unexpected visitor at my room one morning, at the hospital residence. I'd just gotten back from Russ's place with a quarter pound and was diming it up at my desk, when all of a sudden I heard this knock at my door.

I figured, at first, that it was the cleaning staff.

"Yeah, who is it?" I said.

"It's Danzig."

Danzig? I thought.

I didn't think the guy even knew where I lived.

I didn't have a problem with Danzig or anything, so I didn't think much of it. I got up and answered the door.

Danzig had a pissy look on his face.

"What's with you?" I said.

Danzig looked over at my desk. He looked at the weed that I hadn't dimed up yet, which was on top of the desk, and pointed at it. "That's *mine*," he said.

I was baffled. I'd never had a problem with Danzig, the

whole time I'd been selling weed. All of a sudden, out of the clear blue sky, he was at my door, telling me he had some issue with me.

"No, that's *mine*, bro," I said. "I paid for it."

"Well, that was supposed to be for me," Danzig said.

I realized, now, who Russ had been getting his weed from—the same guy who supplied Danzig.

"Buddy, maybe if you paid cash for your shit, it would have been yours," I said. "But you're obviously fronting it. You've been out there longer than I have and you can't fucking pay for your weed? I've been out there *two months*, bud. I've already made a ton of money. I don't need anybody to front me nothing. This shit's mine. I paid for it. Now, get the fuck out of my face."

I slammed the door right in Danzig's face, and then went back to my desk.

The next day, when I went to Russ's place to pick up a quarter pound, I told him about Danzig.

"You know that guy Danzig?" I said.

"Yeah," Russ said. "Sells weeds? Hangs out sometimes in front of the Evergreen?"

"Yeah. Well, he came to my place yesterday. I had my weed on my desk, right? He points to it, as he's standing at the door, and tells me it's his."

"How's it his? You paid cash for it. He fucking fronts it."

"I know."

"So, what did you tell him?"

"I told him to fucking beat it."

Russ laughed. "That guy's pathetic," he said. "He's been hustling weed in front of the Evergreen for almost ten years now, and he still has to front it."

"He's been out there that long?"

"Yeah. He started hustling dimes out there when he was like thirteen years old. He must have some bad habits or something if he's still broke. You'd figure he'd have tons of money in the bank by now."

Russ admitted to me that the guy he was getting the quarter pounds from supplied some of the other street guys who sold weed in the downtown core.

"I knew this guy sold weed to Danzig because he told me one time that Danzig was one of his customers," Russ said.

Russ's dealer obviously had a big fucking mouth on him. Why this guy even talked to his customers about his other customers was beyond me. He'd obviously told Danzig that he was selling to Russ. All Danzig had to do was piece it together. Russ and I were both street guys. We both hung out at the Evergreen to some extent. I was the new guy there. Suddenly, I started selling all of this weed at the same time that Russ started buying quarter pounds off him. I mean, what was two plus two?

It wouldn't have been hard for Danzig to figure out where I lived. Some of the dealers who bought dimes off me knew that I was at the hospital residence. One or two guys had even come up to my room a few times to buy some dimes. I didn't think this would be an issue because I didn't have any problems at the time with anyone on the street. In hindsight, it probably wasn't the best idea.

Russ told me not to worry about Danzig. "That guy's all talk, no action," he said.

"Yeah, you're probably right," I said.

I didn't see Danzig around after that. I figured he just went and fucked off. I kind of forgot about the incident. Then, about a week later, I had another unexpected visitor at my door. It was Moose, Danzig's muscle. He forced his way into my room and then he robbed me.

Moose didn't have a weapon, he was just big. He easily could have beaten the crap out of me if he wanted to. I didn't try to stop him from stealing my stuff because I didn't want to get beat up.

"Did Danzig send you here?" I said, as Moose searched through my dresser. "He came here whining like a fucking bitch the other week."

Moose didn't answer me.

In the bottom dresser drawer, Moose found my stash of toonies and loonies. It was about eighty bucks' worth. I'd been meaning to roll them up and take them to the bank, but I hadn't done that yet. He also found a half ounce of weed.

"Is this all you got?" Moose said.

"Yeah," I said.

"OK. Empty your pockets."

I emptied my pockets onto the dresser. Moose snatched up my wallet and then went through it. There wasn't any cash in it because I'd dropped it all into the bank the night before.

I had a nice wallet. Moose took my ID out of it, tossed the cards onto the dresser, and then put the wallet into his own pocket.

I had my extendable bat in the room, while all this was going on, but I couldn't get to it. Because I'd still been in bed when I'd gone to the door—the knock had come at just after seven o'clock in the morning—I wasn't dressed yet. All I was wearing was a t-shirt and a pair of boxer shorts. If I'd been dressed, I would have had my bat on me, in my back three belt loops. At night, when I slept, I kept the thing under my pillow.

I should have taken the bat with me to the door, when I'd answered it, but for some reason, I'd thought it was the cleaning staff or something. Sometimes they came by in the morning and knocked on the door. I was still half-asleep and I wasn't thinking straight. My brain was all fucking groggy.

If I'd been able to get to that bat, I would have smashed Moose with it. I would have beaten him so hard, I would have put him in the hospital.

When Moose was done going through my desk and my dresser drawers, he searched my closet and under my mattress. In the end, it wasn't a very successful robbery— or home invasion, I should say. He didn't get much, just the half ounce of weed and the toonies and loonies.

On his way out the door, Moose noticed the pair of Adidas running shoes that I'd gotten in exchange for those two dimes of weed. They were on the floor, by my desk.

The shoes were still brand new-looking. I hadn't even worn them yet.

"Fuck it," I said to Moose. "Take the damn shoes."

Moose bent down and grabbed the Adidas. He put them in his bag and then he left.

It was right after Moose left, while I was sitting on the edge of my bed in my underwear, feeling stunned, that I decided to leave Toronto. I'd had enough. I'd struggled so much since I'd gotten stranded in Alabama. I tried to get myself out of a bad situation and to make it on my own in another city. I'd dealt with all kinds of problems, including health problems. It finally looked like I was going to get ahead, and then this shit happened.

Fuck it, I thought.

I just wanted to leave.

I was just tired of everything, really. I was tired of the hustling. I was tired of the street life. I was tired of the fucking city I was living in. I just wanted to go back west to Edmonton, to my home. I didn't want to stick around in Toronto and maybe end up getting beat up, or have something worse happen to me. During my drug dealing days in Edmonton, I'd ended up getting stabbed at one point. I had outstanding drug debts in that city, which is why I'd left town with the show in the first place, but I wasn't worried about those debts now. At the time, I was a seventeen-year-old kid. It had scared me enough to skip town. A lot of time had passed, though, since then. I was older. I knew better. The people that I owed money to could have left Edmonton for all I knew by this point. Or they might have even gotten busted and gone to jail. Either way, I wasn't worried about it. I had money. I could figure something out. I could settle my debts.

Seeing as how Moose hadn't gotten much when he robbed me, it made me feel pretty paranoid, staying in Toronto. I thought, for sure, that this shit with Danzig would escalate. He wasn't going to be satisfied with some coins and some shoes.

I waited until it was nine o'clock in the morning in Edmonton, and then I called my mom. Local time in Edmonton was two hours behind Toronto, so when Moose showed up at my door, it had only been five o'clock in the morning there.

The difference between now, and when I'd called my mom in Alabama, was that I wasn't asking her for money this time. I was just asking for a place to stay when I got into town.

"OK," my mom said, "you can stay here. I hope you're

not just going to stay here until Klondike Days opens in a few weeks, though, and then go back to that stupid carnival."

Klondike Days was a ten-day spot in Edmonton, in mid-July, that Conklin played every year. It was the first spot I'd ever played.

That *first* spot, I thought to myself. What if I'd never played it? What if I'd never gone to the fucking show in the first place?

It had set me on a certain life course, playing that spot. That was for sure. Had I not played Klondike Days in July '92, I never would have left town with the show, and I would have probably never ended up in Toronto, or at least not under these circumstances. I left town because I was running from something. And I was about to leave Toronto because I was now running from something else.

In a lot of ways, I hadn't changed. I was five years older, but I was still the same old Jim.

Going back to the carnival wasn't something I wanted to do anymore. Even though I'd planned to go to the CNE, now that that was definitely not going to happen, I couldn't see myself going back home and then leaving again, by the same means I'd left, five years earlier. It'd be like I'd made no progress. I was still travelling around, living life by the seat of my pants. It had been a crazy ride, an adventure, especially that first year out. But it was time to move on. It was time to do something else.

I told my mom that I wasn't going back to the show. "No, I'm done with that bullshit," I said to her. "It's the reason I ended up in this fucking mess in the first place."

"That's right," my mom said.

"I'm just going to get a job. A *regular* job."

Before I let her go, my mom wanted to know what I'd been doing all this time in Toronto.

"Ah, just this and that," I told her. "First I worked in a clothing store. Then I had this job washing windows."

I didn't go into any further details. The call was long distance, anyhow, so I didn't want to talk much longer.

I told my mom that I'd be leaving Toronto that night on a Greyhound.

"All right," my mom said. "Call me when you get into town. Mike and I will pick you up at the Greyhound station."

Mike was my stepdad.

About an hour after I got off the phone with my mom, the dealers started calling.

"I'm out," I said to each one, and then hung up the phone.

I didn't provide anyone with an explanation. It was none of their goddamn business anyway.

Within a couple of hours, the calls stop coming. There was nothing to do in my room because there was no TV or anything, so for the rest of the day, I just slept.

At eleven o'clock that night, I packed up my shit and checked out of the hospital residence.

On the way to the bus station, I stopped at a bank. I took what I needed for the trip out of the bank machine. Then I headed over to the bus station, on Bay and Dundas. It was only a short walk over there, but it was such a hot and humid night that by the time I got there, with my big duffle bag over my shoulder, I was already sweating.

There was nobody in the line to buy a ticket when I got to the station. I walked right up to the only wicket that was open and told the clerk that I wanted to buy a one-way, advance purchase ticket to Edmonton, Alberta.

The clerk punched the information into his computer. I gave him the money—the ticket was ninety-nine dollars, plus tax—and then he gave me my ticket.

"What time's the next bus to Edmonton?" I said.

"The next bus to Edmonton leaves at 12:07 a.m.," the clerk said. "But you can't leave on that one, sir. That's a twenty-four-hour advance purchase ticket you just bought. You can't leave until tomorrow."

I knew from previous experience that on these advance purchase Greyhound tickets, there was no date of departure listed on them. All they had on them was the date the ticket was purchased and a statement saying that you could only depart on the following day. It didn't say what time, though, on the following day.

"This ticket says that I can leave tomorrow," I said.

"That's right," the clerk said.

"Well, 12:07 is technically tomorrow, ain't it?"

I knew the clerk had no way of justifying it, in terms of the fine print, why I couldn't leave on the next bus. I'd done this so many times with Greyhound and I'd always gotten away with it. I'd always gotten a cheap ride.

The clerk didn't want to argue with me. "All right," he said. "You can take the next bus. But next time, if you're planning on leaving right away, please buy a regular ticket."

"OK," I said.

I left the counter. Then I went to the waiting area and sat down. When it was time to board the bus, I went outside, found my bus, and stood in the line.

In about ten minutes, I boarded the bus. I took a seat at the front.

A few minutes later, the bus left the station. As I looked out the window, taking my last glimpse of downtown Toronto, I realized, suddenly, that I'd never talked to Russ that day. I'd never picked up that quarter pound, so I'd never called him.

Oh, well, I thought to myself. It's too late now.

Russ had really only been an acquaintance, anyway. It wasn't like we'd really been friends. It had been more of a business relationship than a friendship. I still didn't know much about the guy. The whole time I'd known him, he'd never really opened up to me. I'd never even found out how he'd ended up on the street.

I wasn't looking to keep in touch with Russ when I got back to Edmonton. I just wanted to get out of the city and make a clean break from it. Nothing positive had happened to me in Toronto. I wanted to leave it all behind me, honestly.

As the bus headed up Bay Street, I thought about how this was going to be my last long bus ride. After this trip, I was done with the road, I told myself. I was going to go back home, get a stiff job, and for the first time in a long time, I was going to stay in the same place for a while . . .

ABOUT THE AUTHOR

S.E. TOMAS, the "street author," is a Canadian fiction author and former carnival worker who sells his novels on city streets in the Greater Toronto Area. *Squeegee Kid* is his second novel. He lives in Mississauga.

Made in the USA
Middletown, DE
17 March 2017